ENCRATY

ENCRATY

Mystery of the Silver Panflute

MARTEZ ANDREWS II

For Sterling, Solomon, Christa, Kyron,

And anyone who has helped in life.

CONTENTS

1	Tin Foil	1
2	Amnesia	10
3	Amethyst Relic	19
4	The Man with the Linen Shirt	28
5	Summer Solstice	35
6	Lady Monique	40
7	Team Encraty	45
8	Earl Grey Tea	51
9	Cable Men	56
10	Metal Detectors	61
11	Transfer Flight	66
12	Baggage Claim	71
13	Crab Rave	76

14	Christmas Caves	81
15	Abandoned Blade	86
16	Winter's Edge	91
17	Shimmering Leaves	96
18	Pompous Pegasus	101
19	Industrial Improvement	106
20	Unexpected Visitors	111
21	Shadow Seeker	116
22	The Almond Eater	121
23	The Dozers Brotherhood	126
24	Nocturnal World	131
25	The Chase	136
26	Truth Revealed	141
27	The Silver Panflute	146
28	Solemn Song	151
29	Memories Restored	158
30	The Fall of Omar	163
31	Golden Eagle	168

CHAPTER 1

Tin Foil

It was 10:00 a.m., a Friday morning. The sun was glistening through the windowpanes. The morning ravens were chirping eagerly. A gust of wind passed by and embraced a yellow dandelion outside. It was quickly snatched up by a passing adult and discarded.

Devonte was just waking up. He noticed he had set his alarm for 9:00 a.m., but some odd feeling told him to sleep in for an hour. He walked into his bathroom and used a navy-blue toothbrush in the holder near his mirror. It felt strangely unfamiliar as he brushed. Afterward, he grabbed a quick shower. His shower curtain had a foggy, translucent plant pattern depicted on it. The temperature was cold, so he adjusted it more to his liking. It looked unfamiliar. Everything looked unfamiliar.

After getting ready for the day, he walked downstairs to find his mother. She was cooking eggs and sausages into an omelet on a stainless-steel pan. Her dress had a lavender design and flowed gracefully. It flowed as if the summer breeze was present inside the room.

"I know you're just getting up, but be sure to do the dishes before you go out and about," his mother exclaimed. The sink had bowls, a few greasy pots, and two iron pans, all with dried crumbs from last night's family dinner in them.

"Alright, I'll get it done," he responded. He took a small bowl with spinach residue and started. After about an hour, he finished...or so he thought. His 10-year-old little brother, Ethan, placed a dirty bowl of cereal mixed with rice milk into the sink. Following this escapade, he saw his mother staring at him.

"You've finally woken up. We found you unconscious at the park," she said. Devonte looked perplexed.

"How long have I been out?" he asked. His mother grabbed a spatula and flipped the omelet.

"Two whole days. I fed you, and you were still breathing, but I was beginning to get worried," she said. A bewildered expression took on Devonte's face. He paced around near the kitchen countertops for a moment.

"Two whole days? That's crazy!" Devonte exclaimed. "I wonder how I ended up there..."

"Do you remember what happened?" his mother asked.

"I don't seem to remember anything specific," he sighed. He had a slight bruise near his left temple.

"Well, here's what I know," his mother started. "Earlier that day, you texted me and told me that you were out...with a friend, studying or something. You left the house saying that you had to go somewhere. You were in quite a hurry to leave."

"That's interesting. I don't remember sending that text. I also don't remember what friend you are talking about," Devonte sighed.

"You must have hit your head very hard," his mother said. She was now concerned and worried about him. He was acting rather strangely. His behavior was somewhat different than usual. Devonte's stance seemed rigid and stiff rather than loose and jubilant. He was wearing his shoes tied in an unfamiliar knot rather than the typical knot that he usually tied. He was holding a phone in his left hand instead of his right.

"I suppose so," Devonte said. He didn't feel any different, but that was probably figuratively speaking. He did not remember how he was supposed to feel. His mother opened the refrigerator and took out a pitcher of apple juice. She retrieved a tall glass from a pine cabinet and set it down. She then poured the apple juice into the glass and passed it towards him. Devonte now leaned against the countertop with the coldest beverage he had felt in his hand in a long time. His mother had given him an organic brand straight from an apple orchard.

"Well, this juice should help to calm your senses," his mother suggested. She was now zealously preparing the omelet, adding peppers, onions, and garlic seasoning to it. This was an undisclosed family recipe. She had picked it up from a handmade cookbook, passed down to her.

"Thanks," Devonte said as he took a large sip of the cold refreshment. After drinking the juice, he felt slightly better. His left temple was still in pain from the concussion aftermath. Nonetheless, he felt somewhat better. The drink had a pungent refreshing flavor. He could taste the tang of the apple tree from which it had fallen. It renewed his senses and allowed him to allocate his energy towards the beginning of his search to recollect and remember.

Suddenly Ethan walked over to a cabinet.

"Can I have a Pop-Tart mom?" he asked. She looked at him for a second and then nodded yes. Ethan's face lit up with wonder and excitement. Devonte's mother opened the cabinet and handed him a strawberry Pop-Tart. He grasped it in his hand as if he were a college student that had won the lottery. Ethan then rushed off into the living room, proud of his prize. His mother must have been in a good mood.

"Why did you give him that? I thought he had already eaten breakfast," Devonte asked.

"He did a good job on his homework yesterday. I have to be sure to reward that kind of behavior," his mother acknowledged.

"Oh, right," Devonte said, now with slight understanding.

"You should follow his example. Next year, when school comes back around, I also expect you to do well," she added.

"If you get all A's, you just might have a surprise vacation in store." Devonte did not know what she meant by this, but he nodded and said, ok.

He saw a small mural on the wall with a sentence hidden within it. It read, "Family, where life begins." Ethan then turned on the TV. It was deafening. Devonte could hear it all the way from the kitchen. He was watching a nature documentary for kids about whales.

"Hey, can you turn the TV down? It's too loud," their mother exclaimed. Ethan, hearing his mother, then took the remote and pointed it towards the TV screen. He turned it down a couple of notches.

"Is that good?" Ethan asked.

"A little more," his mother said. Ethan then turned it down a few more notches.

"Perfect," their mother said. Devonte stared at the TV for a moment and then headed towards the door. His mother shook her head and called out to him.

"Oh, and Devonte..." his mother said.

"Yes?" his mother responded. He turned around to see a large piece of the omelet she had prepared. She securely wrapped it in a tight bundle of tin foil.

"Take this with you before you leave out. I heard from an article somewhere that eating home-cooking and taking a walk can jog your memory," Devonte's mother said. He gathered his grey backpack, and she gave him leave to venture out. As he went outside, he noticed the abandoned dandelion stem. It was somber and barren. A brief memory flashed across his mind. Devonte remembered a similar situation happening on another occasion. When he was younger, a teenager had plucked a tulip from a community garden. It was on days like these where he secretly went out to plant more.

As he continued walking along the dark grey sidewalk, he looked up. An unexpected sight was there waiting for him. He noticed a large golden eagle with esteemed plumage perched on a powerline above. It stared attentively at Devonte. After fixing its gaze on the tin foil in his hand, it reverted to staring at him. Then, suddenly, it flew off into the distance.

"Well that's interesting," he thought to himself. Usually, golden eagles were not common around city areas. He continued walking.

As he walked, he began to take small bites out of his omelet. It had a distinctive egg and cheese taste. Sadly, he did not remember ever tasting such a food combination. He did not recognize the sidewalk he was walking on, nor the houses on the street. There was a broken traffic light hanging above the road next to his path. The light took longer than expected to change. Cars passed by in a woosh of red and blue. He struggled to carry on without thinking about the consequences of not remembering.

What if he had friends that he made plans with? What if he had an out of town trip he would miss out on? Maybe a concert or a theme park outing was happening without him knowing. He would never know until something stirred his memory, or someone called his name.

"Alright, keep it together," Devonte thought. He then realized there was a slim possibility of him remembering everything all at once. Such a thought made his head hurt. He understood that it would probably take several days to return to his original self, and it made him even more eager to remember. He continued walking. He passed by a group of kids taking turns riding a two-wheeled vehicle.

"Let me use the hoverboard!" One kid exclaimed excitedly.

"Strange," Devonte thought. It did not seem to be hovering. Wouldn't such a vehicle be without wheels? Would it not be levitating above the ground? This was indeed strange.

Soon he approached a crosswalk. There was a brief moment of hesitation before he decided which way he wanted to go. He took a right. As Devonte walked, he felt a chill flow down his spine. A feeling similar to when he remembered how he used to replant the uprooted flowers. A brief flashback flashed across his mind. This street was familiar. It was the same street he used to play on with his best friend.

"What was his name again?" he thought. A clouded version of his friend came into his mind. "A-Alex? No, that can't be right..." He then paced around for a moment. "Allen! That was his name," he almost shouted aloud. Devonte remembered that he was his best friend since childhood. It was on this street that they would go trick or treating. Many summer days were spent over each other's houses playing Halo and Mario Kart. He remembered one occasion where he bet 10 dollars to whoever would win. Sadly, he could not recall the victor. These memories flooded quickly into Devonte's mind; however, he knew this was just the beginning. He had a feeling that he was missing out on so many more memories.

He couldn't describe in great detail what was missing. He just had a feeling in his gut. He probably had forgotten a few past birthday parties or something. Still, he was glad that he remembered the necessary life skills that he needed and was ok enough to think.

"Maybe it will all come back to me later on today," he thought.

There was an immediate improvement in his mood after thinking this. Devonte knew that this was probably just a simple concussion, something mild rather than something serious. He would be ok, and his memories would return in due time if he walked around for a bit.

"Yeah, it's only a matter of time. I'll be fine," he thought. As Devonte walked, he could feel his left temple aching slightly. He began to move towards a large sign. It read: Oak Crossings, in huge dark letters.

"I hope I'm right. I hope he remembers me. I hope we are on good terms," he thought to himself. Devonte's hands were shaking in his pockets. What if this wasn't the right neighborhood? What if he looked like a complete crazy person walking up to a random stranger's home? This was a risk that he would be willing to take.

"I have to remember," Devonte said, now more composed as he steadied himself. He made his way down the sidewalk. It was not a new neighborhood. The houses on the block were decent and well kept, but it was obvious that they were beginning to lose their essence and vitality. The backyard fences of the houses were starting to darken as their birchwood was becoming brittle. Devonte stepped over sections of the sidewalk that were poorly constructed and cracking from deterioration and significant erosion over time.

He then continued until he approached a modest brick house at the end of the street in the subdivision. In the front yard of the estate, was a medium-sized oak tree. Hornets and yellowjackets were zooming by quickly in the summer air. They moved quickly, buzzing from one end of the yard to the next. After collecting himself, he summoned a great amount of courage. Devonte marched towards the house.

Before he could reach the steps, the front door swung open. To his surprise, his hypothesis was correct. This was undeniably the right neighborhood that he had decided to enter. A tall, slender Vietnamese boy, near Devonte's age, hurried out. He was holding an orange Nike box.

CHAPTER 2

Amnesia

From a distance, Devonte knew that this was Allen. Without a doubt, this was the same childhood friend that he had envisioned in his flashback. He was wearing a black Adidas cap and a reflective NASA windbreaker. He remembered that this was the same windbreaker he wore the day they went to the Pacer's NBA game last summer. The low top shoes he wore, were a dark grey color to match his dark grey shorts. As soon as he recognized it was Devonte, he went downstairs to meet him.

"Yo, the new Huaraches colorway just dropped! I copped two pairs the day it was released. Check this out," Allen ranted. A few minutes later, he pulled out a receipt. It was embroiled with thin sharpie writing of markdowns and price comparisons. "The online cartel production ran out of these. You are looking at one of the last pairs produced in the first batch," he said proudly. Devonte looked at the shoes then back at Allen.

"Man, those are fire and all, but not really my style...In fact, I don't really remember my style," he sighed. Allen had a confused look on his face.

"Well, what do you mean by that? You good?" He faltered. Devonte nodded.

"Yeah, I'm alright, just feeling out of it. I must've hit my head two days ago."
Allen still looked puzzled.

"That's mad crazy. How did that happen?" he replied. Devonte shrugged and explained his situation.

"It's tough out here. Have to be safe. I have some ice packs in the freezer if you need one," Allen offered. Devonte accepted and followed Allen inside. He led Devonte to a black refrigerator with a freezer compartment. Allen handed him a blue icepack, and he pressed it against his left temple. It was glacial, but soothing for his aches. He began to feel less anxious, now that he found someone who was with him before the incident. This was someone who he could ask questions. Maybe he even had advice on how he could regain his memories.

"When did all of this start?" Allen asked. He was curious about what had happened to his comrade.

"That's the thing. I'm not really sure," Devonte replied.

"What is the last thing you remember?" Allen asked, with a sense of speculative thought. He was ready to do some detective work to help out his friend in need.

"I don't know. All I know is that I was found in a park, and I was out for two days," Devonte replied. "My mom says I must have hit my head and had a concussion."

"That's mad crazy," Allen responded. He was now walking into his living room. There was a video game console sitting on a coffee table. It connected to the TV with a long HDMI cord.

"One time, I heard that happened to somebody, and they were never the same again," Allen added.

"Well that doesn't help much," Devonte responded. Allen then turned on the TV and selected the console channel using the input button on a nearby remote. He put in a multiplayer racing game disk. They played several rounds, and Devonte lost many times.

"Dang. You forgot how to play too. That's tough," Allen said, as he continued to beat him in the game. Eventually, he got tired of it and was starting to get hungry.

"Man, I'm starting to get hungry. Do you think you could hook me up?" Devonte asked.

"For the sure mane, holdup," Allen said. He then walked into the kitchen. He then looked into the fridge. Inside, there was a pitcher of water, some yogurt that they had just bought, and some leftover hibachi from a family outing they had a couple of days ago.

"Do you like steak? We still have some hibachi left over. You could make a plate," Allen suggested.

"Yeah, that sounds good. Ok, I'll have some," Devonte said. He then walked into the kitchen to scoop some hibachi steak onto his plate. A large portion was left in the box. It was surrounded by vegetables, scrambled eggs, and fried rice.

"Trust me, it was the best hibachi I had ever tasted in my life," Allen said. "I'd rate it five stars out of five. We should go back there for my birthday."

"Alright, sounds like a plan," Devonte laughed. He carried his plate towards their table. It was made of refurbished wood and had a fresh coat of clear gloss, protecting it from scratches or damage. They quickly caught up and hung out for several hours. Allen's mother walked in, carrying a bag of groceries from the all-natural farmers market.

Fresh carrots, tomatoes, and green vegetables were inside of the bag. She had selected the ripest of the bunch, complete with lush leaves and filled with color.

"Hello, Devonte," Allen's mother said in a warm, welcoming tone. She had a grocery list in her hand that she marked up. Vegetable juice, peas, cabbages, she had got everything on the list.

"Hey," Devonte responded in a friendly tone. "Thanks for the hospitality."

"It's the least I could do. I heard about what happened," Allen's mother responded, caringly. "Michela told me about your concussion. I hope any amnesia you have, heals soon."

"I appreciate it," Devonte said. He then continued eating the leftover hibachi steak plate. The meat was tender and had a rich, savory taste. Allen grabbed a cup of pecan yogurt, then took a spoon from their silverware drawer. He ate the cup of yogurt ardently as if it tasted unbelievably good.

"That yogurt was on sale at the store today," Allen's mother mentioned as she set down a bag of groceries. "They are starting a new product line of strawberry-coconut yogurt."

"Sounds delicious," Devonte said. He was now imagining tasting that flavor of yogurt himself.

"May I have one?" Devonte asked with his taste buds interested.

"Sure thing," Allen's mother said. She then took a cup of yogurt out of the fridge for him to eat. He politely thanked her and added it to his meal. After finishing the hibachi, he moved on to the yogurt. It was everything that he had hoped it would be. The strawberry-coconut flavored yogurt had a unique tropical zest.

"I usually don't buy those sugary yogurts from the farmers market, but today I wanted to try something new," Allen's mother said. She began organizing the groceries that she had bought. The vegetables and cold goods went into the refrigerator, canned food went into the cabinets, and snacks went into a big brown pantry closet.

"Well, it was a good idea. This yogurt is delicious," Devonte said. He was now finishing the last of his yogurt. After he had finished, he was ready to throw away his trash.

"Do you know where the trashcan is?" he asked.

"Yeah, come here, let me show you something," Allen said. He led Devonte to a medium metal trashcan with a shiny top. Allen waved his hand above the trashcan, and it opened.

"Woah, that's pretty cool," Devonte said.

"I knew you'd like it. Welcome to the future. It's our new smart trashcan," Allen said proudly. He then discarded the yogurt into the trash.

"Where did you get that?" Devonte asked. He was now curious and wanted one.

"You know the nearest home improvement store. They're not too expensive," Allen said. He then threw away his yogurt and made his way back into the living room. After turning off the gaming console, he put the game back into its case. He also turned off the TV.

"Come, let's go to my room," Allen said. He then led Devonte upstairs. There was a painting of a large red maple tree near his bed.

"I don't know how much you remember, but you gave this to me last year. A university parting gift," he reminisced. He continued to show Devonte things that he thought would help refresh his memory. Allen pulled out an old jersey from when they were on the basketball team and a picture on his phone of them going to a theme park. He even showed Devonte a pair of neon green shoes that he refurbished from their early childhood. All of these possessions showed Devonte things that he already knew. His best friend was a sneakerhead, and he would have to hang with him for a while to learn more about his identity. "You're telling me none of that rings any bells?" Allen inquired. Devonte shook his head.

"Yeah the most I remember are basic things that everyone knows," he sighed. Devonte wondered if the things he remembered were relevant or minute compared to the rest he did not remember. They went back downstairs and spent the rest of the day playing a fighting game. After losing three rounds, he was ready to go home.

"It is getting kind of late," he said. "Maybe tomorrow we can go somewhere and find out more." Piece by piece, they would put his memories back together.

"Sounds like a plan," Allen said. He grabbed a sketchpad from a separate coffee table and put it in his back pocket.

"Yo you know, maybe we could go to the Summer Solstice festival tomorrow," Allen proposed.

"Summer Solstice festival?" Devonte shook his head in bewilderment. Allen then reached out and gave him a flyer from the coffee table. It read, "Summer Solstice festival, 11:30 AM, June 20th. Come by for some fun under the sun."
Suddenly, a new realization occurred. Maybe tomorrow he could meet someone at the festival who knew who he was.

"Alright," Devonte agreed. He gave the flyer back and grabbed his grey backpack. After packing his belongings, he began to head towards the door. As he was heading out, he saw Allen's mother in the living room. She was holding a cyan gardening vase with a small coriander plant inside. Devonte said goodbye to her and left. He thought it best to go directly home. He still didn't know what happened to him at the park or who did it. While he thought about the likelihood of it happening again, his pace began to quicken. Not a full-on sprint but a faster stride, nonetheless. Devonte was determined to reach home before sunset. As he walked more quickly, he passed by the Oak Crossings sign with the large dark letters. Then he passed the crosswalk that he had seen earlier.

Some of the streetlights started to flicker on. Now he knew it was getting late. A few fireflies began to buzz by, calling to each other through the twinkle of the night. The kids that Devonte had seen earlier were now trying to catch them in the palms of their hands. One child had a fairly large jar with small hollows poked through the top of it. "Interesting," he thought. The sun had begun to set. He continued walking. Finally, he arrived home.

"Well, I'm glad I made it home safe," Devonte thought. He reached into his backpack and retrieved a bronze key. He used it firmly to unlock the mahogany wood panel door. It creaked open as he swanned in and closed it behind him. He walked into the kitchen to wash his hands. He was not expecting what happened next. His mother was waiting for him.

"Where have you been? Why are you coming home this late? Do you remember anything yet?" She asked as she bombarded him with even more questions. He hesitated to speak, as he was caught off-guard.

"Well, apparently, I have a best friend named Allen," he calmly said. Devonte's mother then nodded.

"You and that boy have been friends ever since y'all were little. I remember going to the region championship game the other year when your basketball team made the playoffs," she said. Devonte was surprised. He didn't know they went to the playoffs.

"What a day," he thought. He discovered he had a best friend who was a sneaker fanatic, next he found they had made the playoffs together. Devonte told his mother that he still had much to remember. He said to her that it might take a few weeks or even months to recuperate and get his memories back fully. She shook her head in disbelief.

"I give it a week," she said. She told him goodnight and went to bed. Devonte then headed up to his room. His grey backpack slung to the ground as he unloaded a few items that Allen had given him during their hangout. He pulled out a borrowed quartz watch, a borrowed phone charger, and a 10-dollar bill from the bet he had apparently won. He placed the items in the desk drawer beside his bed. He then set out some clothes for the next day. Eager to venture out more, he then went to sleep.

CHAPTER 3

Amethyst Relic

The next morning Devonte arose ready and determined. This time he woke up with his alarm at 8:00 a.m. He went around the house to fill his grey backpack with things he thought he would need on his trip to the Solstice festival. Among his items were a pair of aviators, a few Nutri-grain bars, and a waterproof camera that he had found in his room. As he made it downstairs while gathering these items, his mother walked into the room. She was standing next to his little brother Ethan, holding a toast-brown package.

"Something came in the mail," she professed. Devonte, mystified, accepted the package and brought it to his room to inspect it thoroughly.

"What could this possibly be?" he said as he sat in the chair by his desk and flipped it over. The sender's address was left blank. "Fascinating," he thought. He knew that this meant the sender did not want their address to be discovered by just anyone. This way, if someone went looking for trouble, they would not get very far. After careful consideration, Devonte decided to open it. He lifted it from his desk and into his hands. Then he grabbed a nearby pair of scissors to make a small incision in the package. He believed this would be an efficient way to open a box of this size and shape. Finally, he let loose and tore the package open. What he found next was of the utmost of surprises and wonders. Hidden within the package wrapping were a small amethyst stone and a letter written in cursive. The letter read as follows:

Dear Devonte,

I am giving you this gift not out of fear but of hope. You may not realize what is going on right now or how you were cast into the park. Nevertheless, you must keep trying to remember who you are. This artifact is merely a piece of what you have to learn. It will help you on your journey. I wish I could explain more, but time is of the essence. You must keep going, no matter how tough it may seem. You must stay courageous no matter what dangers may lie ahead. And most importantly, you must remain focused and aware against all the odds you face. You must be ready to overcome them and any foes that may pose a threat. You may not remember much now, but you are a true hero. When the adversities let up, I will be sure to visit you in person, but as for now, keep trying to remember...

Sincerely,

B.,

Devonte was astonished. He read this note several times. He did not know who "B." was or where the package came from, but he did know that this package was important. He probably shouldn't sell the amethyst. It looked ancient and was perhaps vital to whoever sent it. He placed it inside his grey backpack next to the waterproof camera and zipped it up. He then put on the neon-green shoes that Allen had given him the other day. He thought maybe wearing them would help him remember more.

"Let's go get some memories," he thought. Devonte grabbed his backpack and went down the flight of stairs. As he was walking down, he saw Ethan in the living room watching a movie about dolphins. The dolphins were using echolocation for hunting a small school of fish in their pod. His mother caught a glimpse of him as his toe touched the last step.

"Don't forget to clean your room before you go out," she reminded him. He walked back up. Now, this he remembered. He retrieved some supplies that he found in a white cabinet. Among these items was a soapy spray bottle for his mirror, some bleach and cleaning agents for his shower, a brush with a handle, and some disposable latex gloves. Devonte put on the latex gloves.

He started with the sink. He took a spray bottle and cleaned the mirrors with ferocity and haste. He sprayed and wiped it so that there were no smudges or smears left. Devonte then moved to the toilet. He sprayed disinfectant into the bowl. He cleaned it thoroughly, leaving no space untouched. He then moved on to the shower tub. He removed any scum, dirt, or grime that he had found. He made sure to remove any signs of uncleanliness in the bathroom. It was as if he were never there.

After an hour and a half of scrubbing, he was good to go. Devonte removed the latex gloves from his hands. He washed them twice and went into his room. A few moments later, he sat on his bed, pondering the Summer Solstice festival. He wondered if they would have music. He wondered if they would have dancing. He wondered where Allen even got the flyer.

Devonte knew that he needed to go there to learn more about his hometown. He felt restricted and helpless, knowing so little about himself. What if he ran into someone important from his past? If that happened, he would only be able to have a surface level conversation with them. He would be hindered from going deeper and experiencing the strong associations he once had. Just from hanging out with Allen, he knew that he had a lot to remember. He didn't even remember how to play the racing game.

Devonte felt as if he were a newborn babe. He was thrown into a strange world, lacking familiar items and lacking depth through simplicity, the ultimate sophistication. He felt like an alien, on a foreign planet, moved away from his original home, now forgotten. Would he find out who had done this to him? Would the tides of fate reveal the individual who caused him to reach such valleys? Devonte hoped all would be revealed in due time.

He then went back downstairs. He checked the digital clock on the large stove. It was now 9:30 a.m. His generous mother had a small breakfast plate ready for him. On his plate were some grits, eggs, and a small breakfast biscuit. She had heated the plate in the microwave so that it wasn't cold.

"Eat before you head out," she insisted. Knowing that the festival would start soon, he hurried and ate. He wondered what he would remember at the Summer Solstice festival. Maybe he would regain some memories from around this big city. Perhaps he could find someone there who recognized him. He was eager to answer his many questions. He was eager to restore his memories fully. Maybe he would even discover who this "B" person was, from the note that he had found earlier. Devonte headed out the door to find Allen waiting for him.

"Come on. Let's go, man, we're going to miss the Solstice concert," he alleged. Allen was wearing some cargo shorts, a black long sleeve shirt, and a black bucket hat.

"Alright," Devonte responded. They hopped into Allen's small Mini Cooper, and he drove down the street. He put upbeat songs on the radio using his aux cord as he drove along. They moved past their subdivisions and moved deeper into the city. They rode on the freeway for a moment and drove carefully, avoiding lanes clogged with semi-trucks. Allen moved past old sedans and weaved into the fast lane.

Soon they drove off a side road and came off at a city intersection. They moved in a different direction. There was a large green sign directing the ongoing traffic. It read: Downtown Chigaco. After shifting towards downtown, Allen changed the song on his radio, to a more ambient tune. It emphasized the atmosphere that they were entering. As they drove, skyscrapers, monuments, billboards, and museums towered above them. It was a beautiful city with many secrets and curiosities.

"Now this is cool," Devonte said.

"I know right," Allen responded. He was now driving in a more relaxed manner. He liked this scenic route and wanted to absorb all of the scenery thoroughly.

"Look at that!" Devonte said, pointing to a metallic bean-shaped sculpture.

"That? Yeah, the cloud gate is cool," Allen said. He continued driving smoothly.

"We should go out more," Devonte said. He was now more eager to see the expansive world around him that resided in the city's limits.

"What are you talking about, we go out all the—" Allen started, but then looked at Devonte's left temple. Devonte was looking at Allen with a look of annoyance. He had carelessly forgotten about his predicament.

"...Oh yeah," Allen said. The car now got quiet. He drove along with regret and guilt from forgetting such an important detail. How could he not remember such an essential element of the day? His mind became misty with remorse and shame. The car coasted on for a moment. Neither the vehicle nor the road seemed to exist... There were only him, Devonte, and his careless mistake. He decided to lighten the air by giving some words of encouragement.

"Well, I'm sure you'll be back to normal soon, mane. A good festival always puts me in a better mood," Allen said encouragingly.

"Thanks, I hope so," Devonte said. He was still sitting rather quietly in the seat of Allen's Mini Cooper. The words of encouragement were not enough. He still didn't feel so well. There had to be a way to undo his transgression. His friend was in need, and he had made it worse, with his foolish forgetfulness. What would he want if he were in Devonte's position? He had to find a way to help him feel more comfortable. Allen decided to amp his activism up a notch. He would offer a solution that no one could turn down.

"Sometimes I remember the things I forgot about by eating festival food. Food like that can take me back to a different time. Maybe that will jog your memory. Let's just go in there and have a good time," Allen proposed.

"Alright sounds good," Devonte agreed. They passed by a gas station and a few grocery stores. There was a short pause at each red-light where Allen talked about how he had moved to the city when he was very young. He told Devonte about how they used to ride their bikes to the grocery stores to buy candy and sports drinks. He absorbed all of this information as they went along. It was a scenic day outside. The buildings were reflecting sunlight, in a picturesque manner, off of their windowpanes. Allen continued to cruise.

The cityscape's beautiful scenery had taken Devonte off-guard. He took out his camera from his grey backpack. It had a decent amount of free storage space available. He began snapping photos. He captured several aesthetic angles of the city that he planned on revisiting later. He also took a photograph of the city public transportation as it moved along. An intricate network of trams and trains connected the whole city. Abruptly, Allen resumed his questioning.

"Did you remember anything new since last time we met?" Allen asked imprudently.

"Not much," Devonte said.

"Did you do anything different or react to any particular keywords or phrases?"

"Not really," Devonte said. Allen was now getting annoyed with his failure to retrieve an in-depth answer to his questions.

"Did anything interesting at all happen since yesterday?" Allen asked, now belligerently.

"Well I did find a strange artifact in the mail," Devonte declared. He pulled out the amethyst relic. Allen almost skirted off the road. The amethyst looked as though it were precious. It was shaped and fashioned in a way that required accurate exactness and precision. It was refined and polished from the skill of an ancient artisan.

"You're kidding, that's mad wild," he exclaimed. "You know how much that could be worth? Whoever sent that, you need to send them a very personal thank you note." Devonte shook his head.

"I don't think I should sell it, it's probably important. Plus, it came with no sending address," he shrugged. Allen then nodded slowly and let out a hmm. Finally, they had arrived at the festival. He parked his Mini Cooper in a nearby parking lot with a reasonable eight-dollar parking ticket.

"Not bad," Allen said proudly. Usually, good parking spots like this would be difficult to find for special events like this.

However, today was an exception. He claimed a space relatively close. Close enough to where they could hear a resounding beat and see people in the distance smiling and laughing. Devonte wondered if he should bring his backpack inside the festival with him.

After a moment of hesitation and indecision, he decided it would best to bring it. Maybe he would need to use the items he had packed. Or perhaps he would obtain more. It was better to be safe than sorry. Allen pressed a button on his keys to lock his car. He paid for the parking ticket with a crumpled ten-dollar bill he took out of his wallet. They made their way to the entrance. There was a large sign with the words Summer Solstice Festival Today in all yellow capital letters. Standing next to it was a pale young biracial man with curly, brown hair wearing a linen shirt.

CHAPTER 4

The Man with the Linen Shirt

"Pardon me mates, but have you seen a lost dog like this one," the man with the linen shirt said. He then held up a flyer with a fluffy brown Airedale Terrier on it. Devonte and Allen shook their heads.

"No, we just got here. We're here for the festival," Devonte said candidly.

"You're more than welcome to join us. I'm Allen," Allen assured the young man.

"Maybe that little bugger ran off in there. Cheers, I'd be happy to tag along," he agreed.

"Allow me to introduce myself, I'm Ivan," he said.

"What's good, I'm Devonte," Devonte exclaimed. "Yeah, we'll probably find your dog in there if he ran off nearby. He couldn't have gotten far," he insisted.

"Also, go easy on my friend here if he says anything strange, I think he had a mild concussion a few days ago," Allen said.

Ivan then looked sympathetic and assuring. "I'm sorry to hear that, mate. I hope any amnesia you have goes away soon," he said. They each assumed that hopefully, they could help one another. Devonte could restore more of his lost memories, and Ivan could find his beloved lost fluffy Airedale Terrier. Together, the three of them walked inside. It was very colorful. People were dancing to overhead music playing from a live band, eating cotton candy, and trading sunglasses at small vendor stations. Devonte caught sight of a small child running around with a sun-shaped bubble wand. There were three bounce houses with palm tree themed decorations on them and one that was a big yellow slide.

As they walked deeper into the festival, Ivan noticed that the music had changed. The song had gone from a slower jazzy tune to an up-tempo familiar song.

"Oh, I know this song. I heard this melody at a rave, back when I lived in the UK," he said happily. Ivan was smiling in disbelief as he didn't think Americans would know this song. Allen was also captivated by the upbeat tune.

"Yo, this goes hard," Allen agreed as he began nodding his head steadily to the beat.

"We have to stay focused," Devonte said. He had a feeling that if they got sidetracked, they might lose the Terrier and not make much progress finding his memories. Allen glared at him as if this was an example of him saying something out of the ordinary.

"It'll only be for a second. I'm sure we can have a little fun," Allen said positively.

"Oh, come on, I'm really feeling it," Ivan said. After some moderate coaxing, Devonte finally changed his mind. They slowly made their way through a crowd towards the concert stage. Hundreds of people were there. They were jamming and dancing to the music, now amplified and booming through the loudspeakers. As they walked into the concert area, a man in an orange Suns jersey was tumbling and doing flips outside of the main crowd. There was a DJ with a shiny reflective helmet operating some large, monochrome, neon blue turntables. The boys saw a group of girls near their age, and they began to dance.

Devonte was surprised that he still knew how to dance. This was one of the few things he recalled, without needing a reminder. As the music flowed, his body moved and swayed flawlessly with the clamorous beat. His dance partner reflected his dance moves and smiled back at him. After a little while, they became almost completely in sync. As he moved forward, she moved back with prodigious footwork, her hips mirroring his movements. A dance circle began to form around them.

The music began to ascend into a crescendo. Devonte started to dance more intensely as if an outside force guided him. They built up the dance with the music until the beat dropped. Their motions flowed and streamed with the change of the rhythm. Soon the song was over, and the music went back to normal. He and the girl stared at each other for a moment.

"Hey, I'm Nicole," she revealed. She looked at him with a warm smile and seemed nice.

"I'm Devonte," he responded. He then took out his phone, and they briefly exchanged numbers. Just then, Allen caught a glimpse of Devonte's watch. The time was now 11:30 AM.

"We should probably get back on it," Allen said reluctantly. He motioned for them to come on, as they had to continue searching. Allen grabbed some cotton candy from a nearby stand. They moved away from the stage area. As they were walking away, Nicole made the call me motion with her hand towards Devonte.

"Where'd you learn to dance like that mate? You were killing it out there," Ivan said. Devonte shrugged. He had a hard time believing this himself.

"Don't know, just did it," he said. He was standing to the side with a calm and collected demeanor.

"Ah, you got some game. That girl was feeling you," Allen teased. He patted Devonte lightly on the back.

"Let me remember some things first before I jump to conclusions. For all I know, I may be taken," Devonte laughed. They moved towards the festival food area of the event. There they saw solstice-themed hamburgers and taco dishes, as well as snacks like pretzels and bags of popcorn. Ivan and Devonte grabbed a plate, and the three sat down at a round metal table. A few umbrellas were above these to shield them from the sun's intense rays. Devonte took a large bite out of a taco. It was filled to the brim with jalapenos, beef, lettuce, and cheese.

Ivan had spent his money on a double-stacked juicy Angus burger. There was bacon, lettuce, tomatoes, and guac packed tightly into two very thick seeded buns. As he bit into the toasted bread, his mouth watered with the succulent, fulfilling taste of the sandwich.

"That burger looks good," Devonte said. Although he had a taco, it was not nearly as dense as Ivan's burger.

"It is good," Ivan said.

"Alright, so here's what we know," Allen started. "A few days ago, my best friend over here, woke up with no clue of who he was, or what had happened to him. He definitely must have hit his head, because he didn't even remember us making the playoffs."

"And we have this," Devonte reminded. He pulled out the violet amethyst relic.

"Woah, now that's a beauty," Ivan said. "If only it could help me find my dog."

Just then, an unforeseen calamity took place. His hand lurched suddenly from its once fixed position. Must have been a reflex that had activated in the remedial process. It happened so quickly that his currently stagnant mind could not comprehend or perceive the action. Before he could catch it, a piece of his taco fell to the ground. It fell as if it were in slow motion. The ingredients of the taco dislodged themselves from the cheese and the shell. This was a rather unexpected accident. As it took place, Devonte visibly had a change of attitude.

"Aw, that's just great," he almost swore. This happened in the most untimely of moments. He thought that he needed the food to rejuvenate his memories and help him to think more clearly. Instead of resting at the bottom of his stomach, the food was now resting on the ground. At that moment, to everyone's surprise, a brown Airedale Terrier came out of nowhere. He was quick and nimble, scurrying towards them with the ever most speed and velocity. It began to gobble up the piece of his taco. Devonte's catastrophe had become the dog's dinner.

"Quick! Grab 'em!" Ivan exclaimed. He pulled out a blue leash from his right pocket. He planned on using it to apprehend his Terrier. He would snatch the scoundrel from his charade and end his mischief, with rigid resolve and unchanging great haste. Devonte got up from the table and slowly walked toward the dog. Allen was on the other side, blocking its escape. After the careful cornering of the Terrier, Ivan pounced. He captured his once unrestricted canine and attached the blue leash to his matching blue collar.

"Gotcha! Think you could run from me, aye Fluffy?" He laughed. The dog whined but accepted defeat in his game of "hide and seek."

"That's your dog?" Allen said, surprised.

"Yeah, that's my fluffy. Curious little fella, isn't he?" Ivan said. He was now rubbing his Terrier behind the ears. He had wandered off too far from home and was now found. Ivan was thrilled that he had found his way back to him. He would not have to go to the office store to print out 200 lost dog signs that he would hang around the city. He would not have to rant on social media posting lost dog tweets or blog posts. Fluffy would be well taken care of, back in the supervision of Ivan.

Ivan was an overprotective owner who would do everything in his power to keep his Terrier safe. Whether that meant pampering him and training with expensive dog whisperers or walking through 106-degree weather on the summer solstice, Ivan was always ready.

"Well, one problem solved. Thanks for your help," Allen said. He was in disbelief of such luck. They had found the mangy mongrel, without having to exert much energy. Devonte, who was surprised as well, now had a grin on his face. He hoped they would be able to recover his memories with such haste and rapidity.

"If it's alright with you, I'd like to keep tagging along. You've helped me, and I'd like to help you in return," Ivan insisted.

"Yeah, you can stay," Devonte said as he put the relic away. Allen, Ivan, and Devonte continued exploring around the festival. They saw sun-shaped pottery, candy, and kites for sale. All of this was overpriced and unrealistically expensive.

"Guess I won't be buying any solstice gear," Allen said with a gloomy saddened tone. "All of these snacks are just as expensive as snacks in the movie theater." They then heard the sound of drumming and traditional music in the distance. The solstice would start soon.

CHAPTER 5

Summer Solstice

They edged closer to where the sounds where coming from. It seemed like the festival was about to take on an even better turn. The kids, running around with sun-shaped bubble wands, began to join their parents. People were gathering towards a city street with two metal blockades on the sides of it. It was as if everyone were anticipating something. Eight security guards were standing on alert just in case.

Just then, a large orange parade float appeared from behind the corner of a building. It was sun-themed. Performers in colorful outfits were standing and waving on it. There were fire jugglers, and mascots dressed up in fancy orange costumes. There were even two people on stilts adorned in decorations walking tall and wobbly behind it. Several other floats followed it. A man in a carrot-orange top hat emerged from inside the first float. He was holding a megaphone.

"Today is a historic day for our city! It marks the 20th annual Summer Solstice festival!" he roared proudly. A few of the performers had tambourines and were making music in style. There were more musicians with trumpets and trombones, all perfectly in sync and playing a harmonious tune. They proceeded to enter the center of the festival with great pride and esteem.

Kids at the festival were oo-ing and ah-ing at such a sight to behold. Allen, Devonte, and Ivan were near the front of the crowd close to the long metal barricades. Suddenly, Devonte felt a sharp pain in his temple. He put his hand on his head for a moment. A brief memory flashed across his mind.

He was in a stroller in what seemed like another big city. In his flashback, there were many digital street billboards. One of them read, "New York City: The world's second home." He then saw a large digital clock counting down. 10...9...8...7...It continued to count down. Thousands of people were counting down with it.

Devonte saw a younger version of his mother. There was also some shadowy, foggy figure close to her that he couldn't make out. 3...2...1... It went on. Once the countdown had reached its end, a huge sound roared, and a colossal sphere dropped, releasing thousands of balloons in every size, shape, and color. The assortment looked as if it were forged straight out of a cartoon or animated film. Then he felt a hand on his shoulder that snapped him back into the present.

"Yo, you good?" Allen inquired.

"Yeah, you must've taken a nasty hit to the head the other day," Ivan chuckled. This was most definitely the case.

"Yeah, I'm straight," Devonte responded. The parade continued. A Jazz band started playing another upbeat harmonious song. A brunette in a tan fedora was singing next to a tall man with an indigo bass guitar. The crowd was loving every second of it. Community events like these took place regularly. These happenings were spectacles of awe and wonder as they inspired feelings of joy and happiness. A girl holding a yellow balloon was pointing and smiling at a large inflatable sun-shaped float up ahead. Her mother was also smiling.

Bursts of red and orange confetti were shooting out of a confetti cannon. The streets were beginning to be ornamented in confetti. The many parade floats began to move towards a rotunda. They circled it and continued slowly, as festival guests and citizens were taking pictures and admiring their craftsmanship and effort. The man in the carrot-orange top hat with the megaphone was now also waving and smiling at bystanders.

Devonte caught sight of a man making his way towards the front of the parade float. He had a thick mustache and was wearing a grey collar shirt with matching grey gloves. Abruptly, Devonte felt a disturbing vibration. He looked down and saw a glow, with a faint violet hue, emerging from his left pocket.

"That's strange," Devonte thought. "It doesn't usually do that." Allen and Ivan also began to notice the violet glow, as it was getting even brighter.

"Yo, has it always done that?" Allen said anxiously.

"No, not...that I know of..." he replied. "I think we should go before someone notices." The security guards were posted up. They were on the lookout for any signs of trouble or distractions from the main event. The man in the grey collar shirt was coming even closer into view. He was holding a cane with a jade gemstone on the tip of it. As the parade float moved closer, he was nearing the front of it. Devonte felt a disturbing feeling in his chest, along with increasing vibrations of his amethyst relic. The relic was pulsing, almost as if it had a heartbeat.

"Yeah, we should go. I don't feel so well," Devonte muttered. Ivan also felt uneasy about it all.

"Yeah, mate, you don't look so good. Let's get out of here," he said tentatively. His Terrier barked curiously. Suddenly, a young woman with dreadlocks and circular glasses approached them. She had dark cocoa skin and was wearing a lab coat.

"There's no time to explain. Come with me, I'll explain on the way," she imparted. Without asking questions, the three followed her out of the crowd. They walked past the barren vendor stations. They walked past the bounce houses that were now gradually deflating. They made their way into the parking lot. Next by Allen's Mini Cooper was now a dark, lavender Lexus.

"Please follow me. My lab is not far from here," she said. She then went into her car.

"Um alright," Devonte responded.
Ivan let out a deep breath. "I hope it's ok if my dog comes too. We walked here," he said.

"I have a spare beach towel under the seat, yeah I guess it's alright," Allen sighed. The three piled in Allen's Mini Cooper and buckled their seatbelts. The fluffy Terrier was panting eagerly.

"Maybe she knows more about the amethyst relic," Devonte thought. She hopped into her lavender Lexus and started the engine. She took a brief turn out of her parking space and drove off hastily. They began to follow her in Allen's Mini Cooper. As she was driving, she made two sharp left turns and a right. Surprisingly, all of the stoplights were green on the trip. Her lavender Lexus reflected magnificently against the glass windows of buildings and the bases of skyscrapers with high elevations.

Finally, they arrived at a small apartment-like building. The young woman with the dreadlocks practiced the utmost care while parallel parking. Allen parked similarly behind her vehicle. Ivan, Devonte, and the Terrier came out with wonder and curiosity. She opened the door carefully as if she were being watched.

CHAPTER 6

Lady Monique

She climbed the stairs to the door and reached into her lab coat. She pulled out a bronze key similar to the one Devonte had. She unlocked the door then put her thumb on the doorknob. The boys looked confused. Then a robotic voice initialized.

"Who dares to enter?" It bellowed.

"Lady Monique, daughter of Nefertiti," she responded. A metal unlocking sound reverberated, and the door mechanically moved open. Allen and Devonte looked at each other with expressions of both curiosity and caution. Ivan was speechless and astonished. They walked inside. The door was wooden on the outside but metallic when seen from within the lab. It gradually closed behind them. Where there was supposed to be a lobby area, there was a large chamber containing shelves with multicolored beakers on them. On the walls, there were paintings of Ancient citadels and fortresses. Ivan tied his Terrier's leash to a conveniently placed coat hanger drilled into the floor. He fed him some dog treats. The group walked into a small violet room with a low round table and pillows surrounding it.

"Thanks for trusting me and coming on such short notice," she acknowledged. "My name is Monique. I can tell you more about the relic in your possession, Devonte," she proclaimed with certainty. Again, Devonte looked surprised. He did not remember telling her about the amethyst relic. He also did not remember telling her his name.

"You...must know who I am," he responded.

"Have a seat," she offered. Allan, Ivan, and Devonte each took a pillow surrounding the table. Monique also sat down. On it was a tablet with a purple keyboard case. She turned it on. It was fully charged. She went into her camera roll. On it was a picture of several ancient documents, some dating from the age of the Macedonian empire.

"I am what you may call an archeologist. I have been studying many ancient texts and transcripts for quite some time now," Monique continued. "The amethyst relic in your possession dates back to almost 50 centuries ago." Ivan looked astonished.

"Well, never mind then. We should keep it," he reformed. Devonte reached into his pocket and pulled out the amethyst relic. It was no longer glowing.

"How did you know I was carrying it? Let alone, how did you know where to look for us there in that large crowd," Devonte inquired warily.

"I was there when you hit your head," Monique said with a laugh. "You probably don't remember me yet, but we are on the same side. That relic is one of the important ancient relics from the ancient world. Formally it is known as the Amethyst of Akhenaten." She retrieved a small mechanism from her desk. It looked like a tracking device of sorts.

"Each relic gives off a faint, distinct radiofrequency. I have designed this device to pick up each frequency and ultimately help in my search and recovery mission. My mission is to protect the relics from falling into bad hands," she continued. Monique began swiping through her tablet. In her camera role were drawings that looked very archaic and dated. Allan, Ivan, and Devonte saw that the images, shown at various angles, consisted of several other items. Displayed were a golden necklace, a dark red glove, a bronze ring, a blue amulet, and a sparkling silver panflute.

"These are the mythical vestiges of the ancient world," she said. She then began pointing at the images with inspiration and awe. "This is the fabled Necklace of Nefertiti. It is said to give its wearer the ability to detect fallacies and see-through facades. I read from a scroll. It is supposed to be buried along a deep ancient river. I've been trying to track it, but my scanner's range must not go far enough yet," She sighed. "This is the renowned Eagle Gauntlet of Genghis Khan. It is said to give its user the ability to call any bird at will and command them," She went on. Allen was intrigued.

"Yo, that would be mad crazy if I could to that," he said enthusiastically. Devonte listened carefully. This conversation was starting to pique his interests. Ivan scooched in closer.

"You mean to tell me there's more of these?" he said. "That's fascinating."

"Yes, indeed," She continued. "This is the Runic Ring of Lady Boudica. It is of Celtic origin and is said to give, whoever is brave enough to wield it, extreme courage and the ability to lead great armies." Monique kept swiping on her tablet.

"Next is the Amulet of Hatshepsut. It is said to be given to her by her father. In theory, it can give one special healing abilities and the power to control the weather or rapidly cultivate any form of vegetation," she exclaimed.

"Now that would be a superpower," Devonte thought to himself. He pondered growing apple trees for homeless people.

"The Amethyst you hold in your hand is said to radiate when danger is nearby. It is also said to give its users the ability to project powerful blasts of ultraviolet light," she reckoned. Devonte looked at the amethyst. It was still dormant. Maybe that was why it was glowing then at the Summer Solstice parade. Was he in danger? Did it have something to do with the man in the grey collar shirt? He had many questions.

Suddenly, Monique began to talk in a quieter tone, as if there were microphones in the walls, implanted by secret agents, recording their whole conversation.

"And finally, is the most important relic of all the ancient relics, the legendary Silver Panflute. It is said to be an object of great aptitude," she spoke.

"Legend tells it was once held by the majestic Cleopatra," Monique began again. "It was given to Caesarion, the often-unmentioned son of the prodigious power couple, Julius Caesar and Cleopatra," Monique went on. Ivan was thrilled.

"Woah! So, he's like me, aye?" he blurted.

"The Silver Panflute is said to have a unique ability that is far more powerful than all the other relics. I haven't been able to learn much about it, but I know it exists and holds many secrets," she resumed. "Devonte, you joined my team a year ago. You probably still don't remember much, but we come from the same bloodline. We are descendants of Nefertiti."

"Interesting," Devonte muttered. Suddenly a brief memory flashed across his mind. This one felt oddly different from the others. He was standing in a desert field. There were bushes scattered across, and it was a clear night. Devonte could make out two figures in the distance. They were standing among a circle of stones that resembled a rugged sundial. As his memory got clearer, he could perceive the two figures better. It looked like a father and his son. The taller figure was pointing towards stars in the sky. Devonte then awoke from it.

"You alright, mate?" Ivan asked mockingly. Devonte then sharply snapped out of it.

"Yeah, sure," he replied. Monique then turned off her tablet. The group was now more awakened and more informed than when they entered.

CHAPTER 7

Team Encraty

Allen pulled out an old reebok receipt and a blue ink pen from his right pocket.

"I'm going to need to jot this down just in case I forget," he said. He scribbled the names of the relics that Monique mentioned. He also drew rushed pen drawings of the gold necklace, amethyst, dark red glove, bronze ring, blue amulet, and the sparkling silver panflute. He then put the receipt back into his pocket. Ivan was now staring at a globe on a mahogany shelf, in the corner of the room.

"Can you bring that over here, please?" Monique asked as she saw Ivan looking at it.

"Sure thing," Ivan said. He stood up and carried it over towards the table. A few colorfully assorted sticky notes were attached to it, in several different locations. The sticky notes were placed pointing towards Cairo, Alexandria, and Memphis, Egypt. There were also sticky notes on Mongolia and Britannia.

"If my sources are correct, I believe the Silver Panflute is located at Christmas Island, near Australia," she said.

"Hey, I know that island," Ivan almost shouted. Earlier, he had thought today would be an average day. However, it was becoming quite extraordinary. Not only did he find his Terrier, but he found new friends who were interesting and exciting.

"Well what are we waiting for?" he said eagerly. Allen was also beaming with anticipation.

"I'm glad I got my passport last year," he smiled enthusiastically.

"Yeah mate, the world is a big place. As I'm from the UK, I always keep mine on me," Ivan said proudly. He took out a passport in a velvet red leather case. It had stamps stamped on it of London, Greenland, Rome, and other places in Europe. Devonte took the medium grey backpack from his back and unzipped it. There was no passport in it, however, in a pouch he hadn't checked until now, there was an old airline ticket. A surprised look took on his face instantaneously. It read: BW10 6:15 A6 201, Caribbean Airlines Boarding Pass.

"Well this is new," Devonte testified. He then proceeded to text his mother, asking if he had a valid passport. Almost immediately, she texted back.

"Yeah, we went to the Caribbean last year. Why?" She faltered. Devonte started texting and explaining all that had happened.

"Oh, well, I'm glad you've met some new friends," She responded. The three text ellipses were moving rapidly. "Just make sure you don't spend all your allowance. You still have money left over from back when you won that big scholarship from that fancy science program. It covered school but don't waste the rest, save some of it for a rainy day," She suggested. Devonte was ecstatic. This was the best news that he had heard all day. Now he knew he would be able to join the group on such an adventure.

"Yep, I can come. How are we going to get flights there and back?" Devonte inquired. That moment Monique took out a travel visa in a navy-blue case. It looked rather recent.

"Let's just say...I know a guy," she grinned.

"We should have a name that we call ourselves," Monique suggested. Allen stared up at the lavender ceiling.

"Maye the relic sleuths," he proposed.

"That doesn't really roll off the tongue," Ivan shook his head. "How about the artifact army? That has a nice ring to it," Ivan suggested. Monique shook her head.

"We don't have an army or the artifacts, stay focused," she said. Devonte's looked as if he was deep in thought.

"That's it," Devonte exclaimed, as he had an epitome. "Can you say that one more time?"

"What? Army?" She alleged.

"No, after that. You said something else," he said. She looked very confused and wondered what he wanted.

"Stay focused?" Monique said quizzingly.

"Yes. That's it. Focused," Devonte replied. He remembered a word that he had heard from somewhere. He pulled his phone back out. He opened a search browser and hastily typed in the word Encraty. Multiple definitions popped up.

"Encraty, to be in control of one's desires or actions. Encraty, mastery over the senses. Encraty, abstinence from pleasures of sense; Encraty, self-control," he read aloud. Allen, Ivan, and Monique looked at him for a brief moment.

"I like that," Allan remarked.

"Not too shabby, mate," Ivan agreed.

Monique nodded. "Perfect," she said. "That's the Devonte, I remember." Devonte didn't know what she meant by this but did not complain. He knew she probably knew more about his backstory than he knew himself. As of now, nothing was stopping them. Allen, Ivan, and Monique were all excited and prepared to make the trip to Christmas Island. They walked out of the violet room and back into the large chamber with multicolored beakers. There was a brief pause in their steps as Ivan caught sight of his Terrier. He was scratching at the door, trying to escape again.

"Now, where do you think you're going?" he chuckled. Ivan undid the leash from the coat hanger and gave his Terrier some more dog treats.

"It would probably be best if we went out the back door," Monique suggested skeptically.

"I have something I have to pick up, and it's back there." On their way out, they passed by a table with a large beaker with a blue liquid inside it. Next to it was a pack of plastic cups.

"Would you like a sip?" she offered as she picked the beaker up.

"No thanks," Devonte politely retorted. "I have common sense," he thought. Allen grabbed a plastic cup, and she poured some of the liquid inside of it.

"I sure am thirsty," Allen exclaimed. He glugged it down without asking any questions. Ivan also refused the beverage. Allen then looked worried. The beaker began to fizz.

"Wait. What? Will I get sick or something?" he asked. He now began overreacting. "Will I...die? Who will take over my shoe collection?" he panicked.

"No, it's just blue Gatorade mixed with sprite," Monique laughed. I discovered this fantastic combination one day when I was at a gas station. She poured herself a cup and took a sip. Allen let out a huge sigh of relief.

"Oh, I was about to say...I thought I was going to have to sell my supreme gear to pay a doctor's bill," he joked. They then proceeded towards the back of the room, where there was a metal door similar to the front door.

There was a small coffee table with two books and a wrapped piece of parchment paper. Monique unwrapped the parchment paper to reveal a small map with markings on six locations similar to the globe that they had seen earlier. Using a black sharpie, she marked Christmas Island and crossed out Mongolia. She then folded it and secured it tightly into her right lab coat pocket. She then tapped in a 9-digit passcode on the complex passcode lock. The metal door mechanically creaked open. They were now standing in what seemed like a back alley.

CHAPTER 8

Earl Grey Tea

The door closed. Devonte checked his watch. The time was now 5:30 p.m. The alley they were in was grimy and unkempt. They began making their way towards their parallel parking spaces. As they were walking, a stray cat appeared from behind a green trashcan. It meowed then scurried away. Monique pulled out a cellphone with a violet case. She briefly dialed a phone number. As it was ringing, she motioned everyone to come closer.

"This is my plane guy," she said. After a couple of rings, someone with a soft but raspy voice answered.

"Walter, it's me. We went to Barbados together," Monique responded.

"Oh, Monique! It's been a while...Long time no see," the voice roared. "What do you need?" he asked.

"Do you think you can get us to a place called Christmas Island?" Monique inquired.

"But of course, my lady. Let me see what flights I can book," he responded. There was a brief pause as the person on the other line was searching for flight times.

"Oh, I know this island. My cousin used to live there," he added. The group heard a few sharp keyboard sounds coming from the phone. "So, is it just you? How many are we talking about?" The man asked.

"There's four of us in total. Oh, and there's a dog," Monique replied.

"Don't think I can allow pets on this flight," he sighed.

"However, I think I can make do with the four of you all...Sounds exciting," he ranted.

"Alright, that works fine," Monique responded. She then said, "See you soon" and hung up. Ivan looked at his Terrier and frowned.

"Guess I'll have to find a dog sitter for you fluffy," he said.

The Terrier began panting excitedly. Allen also texted his mother, clarifying everything. He explained that he had made new friends and wanted to go on a brief trip for a few days. She was all for it as she would be spending that week experimenting with her garden. They kept walking towards their parallel parking spaces. The group moved around debris and old fast food bags. As they were walking, they all exchanged phone numbers and created a group chat. Finally, Allen, Ivan, and Devonte made their way towards the Mini Cooper. Monique walked towards her Lexus.

"We should meet again come autumn, in the same place. By then, I should have tickets, so pack wisely," Monique mandated.

They nodded ok and piled in the Mini Cooper. Ivan's Terrier sat on the towel again. He then whimpered, gloomily.

"Stay safe!" Monique called out to them before she sped off.

"Alright, where did you say you lived again?" Allen said as he pulled out his phone to open a map app.

"Not far, I live a few blocks off Lincoln Park," Ivan said. Allen passed his phone so that he could input his address. Ivan then entered it in hastily. They drove off towards the location.

The community they went to was clean and well kept. Only an occasional street mural or endorsed wall graffiti stood out from the ordinary scenery. These were scattered evenly adorning the neighborhood with colorful paintings of animals and peaceful settings. There was a small park nearby with people walking their dogs and throwing frisbees. Ivan's Terrier stared out of the window with anticipation as they drove. Finally, they arrived at a modern apartment complex.

Lush bushes were sprouting from designated sections of the building. The apartment was about seven stories high, with an orange coat of paint spread across it. Ivan, Allen, and Devante hopped out of the Mini Cooper and walked up the stairway to his apartment door. Ivan took a bronze key from out of his pocket and motioned it towards a bronze keyhole. It unlocked. A flock of pigeons flew overhead.

"Nasty buggers those are," he mumbled. He then motioned for them to come in. As he closed the door, Allen and Devonte could see him initiating a phone call with a potential pet sitter. His apartment was spotless as if it were just recently built or refurbished. Ivan walked to the kitchen to wash his hands. He grabbed a small pitcher of water from the fridge and poured some of it into a large dog bowl. The bowl was turquoise and had the word fluffy on it in big, bold letters. His Terrier walked towards it and began to sip, excessively. While on the phone, Ivan opened a cabinet and took out a green mug. He then moved the phone away from his head and pointed towards something on the counter.

"Can you hand that box to me, mate?" Ivan said. On the countertop was a small box that read, "Twinings of London: Earl Grey Tea Since 1706." Devonte handed him the box.

"Cheers," he said as he took a packet out and continued to negotiate on the phone with the pet sitter. Allen looked out a window and saw another stray cat like the one at Monique's lab.

"Nice neighborhood," Allen smirked. Devonte gave him a look. After 10 minutes, they could see Ivan wrapping up the phone call with his sitter.

"Alright ill drop little Fluffy here off, Monday afternoon. Have a good evening," he agreed to and then hung up. Ivan inserted the tea packet into the green mug. He then added warm water and used a small teaspoon to blend it. Devonte then looked at the tea. "You should try some, it'll calm your nerves," Ivan offered as he handed Devonte the mug.

"So that's Earl Grey tea, huh?" he asked. Small puffs of smoke were pouring out of the mug. He took a small sip; it had a bittersweet taste. Surprisingly it did seem to calm his nerves. His head felt a little better as he continued to drink it. Allen looked at Devonte and nodded as if to say Ivan was approved. He was turning out to be a very admirable friend, indeed. They thanked him for the hospitality and headed out the door.

"We should come early next Wednesday, so we have a heads up on the group," Allen said. "That way, they can't say we were late."

"Sounds like a plan indeed," Devonte agreed. They climbed into Allen's Mini Cooper and headed back to their side of town. On the way, Allen was blasting a new reggae song that he had found the other day. Allen was one interesting guy. As they arrived at Devonte's house, it was starting to get dark out. He waited patiently, as Devonte stepped out with his grey backpack.

"See you Wednesday, my guy," he then said and drove off. Devonte walked towards his house, holding the amethyst relic firmly in his hand.

"Well at least I know what it does now," he thought to himself. As Devonte entered his driveway, something unexpected began to happen. The amethyst was glowing.

CHAPTER 9

Cable Men

Devonte looked around and noticed a grey van, with a green decal slogan on it, parked near a sidewalk. The logo on it read: Oze: Business Class Cable and Ethernet.

"That's odd, I don't remember mom saying we needed to have the cable fixed," Devonte thought. He then walked inside. In the living room, he saw two buff men in grey polo shirts with the Oze logo. They were adamantly installing what looked like a new cable box. There was also a uniquely-shaped remote that came with it. The cable men gently lifted the TV. This was the same TV that Ethan was using to watch the dolphin movie earlier.

"Look Devonte, we just won a free cable box from one of those late-night radio shows," Devonte's mother said. "Their set up is so first-class," she said with a smile.

"Ma'am, we're happy to help," one cable man said. He then plugged in an HDMI cord to the box. The other cable man caught sight of Devonte. He had a menacing grin.

"That looks suspicious. Is this why the amethyst was glowing?" Devonte thought. The cable man then walked closer to Devonte.

"Son, we've just installed a state-of-the-art cable box, free of charge. It's one of the few newer models we have in stock. You're about to experience unbelievably high-quality television on your retina display," he went on. In his hand was a device that looked similar to the one Monique had earlier. However, it did not look as advanced as hers. As he was explaining, he did not seem to be fully present. It seemed as if he were scanning the room, searching for something.

"If your cable ever goes out, we'll be back to help," the man said. He handed Devonte a metallic business card. It read: Jim Myers prepping electronics and appliances since '69. Jim looked at Devonte watchfully as he read the business card.

"Glad to have you with us," Jim said, almost mechanically. Devonte felt the disturbing pulse in his left pocket intensifying. Soon the man working on the TV was finished.

"Okay, Jim, the Oze box is installed and ready," he bellowed. He then packed the items they didn't use into a box.

"Mike, I think we're done here," Jim said. He took the box from Mike, and they headed towards the door.

"You two have a good evening," he said with a grin. They stepped out the door and got into their van. They then drove off, with a sense of great authority. Devonte stood in the doorway baffled.

"Who were those guys really?" he asked himself. He then checked his pocket. The amethyst relic was no longer glowing.

"Devonte, come do the dishes!" His mother called out to him. He slouched and apathetically strolled over towards the sink. There were only a few dishes in the sink this time. It was only a large pot with cooking grease in it and some plates. He finished them and then went to bed.
The next morning came. Devonte woke up and checked the clock. It was 9:30 a.m.

"Interesting, woke up an hour and a half later than usual," Devonte thought. He showered, brushed his teeth, then put on khakis and a grey-striped collar shirt. Although he did not have his grey backpack on, he was ready for the day. He walked downstairs. As soon as he walked downstairs, he saw the Oze box blink a green light. It then went dormant.

"Well, that's strange," he thought. Devonte's mother came out of her room.

"You ready? It's Sunday morning. We're about to head to church," she said. Ethan was already dressed in his "Sunday best."

"Can I eat cereal, mom?" Ethan asked. "Yes, go grab a baggie from the pantry, and I'll get some cheerios from out of the cabinet," she agreed. Devonte's mother gave Ethan his cereal. She then pulled car keys from out of her purse and led him outside, into her car. Devonte, wearing his khakis and collar shirt, followed. The vehicle was a green Tahoe. He hopped in the passenger seat and buckled his seatbelt. Ethan was munching on cheerios in the back of the Tahoe.

"Buckle your seatbelt, Ethan. We're going to be late!" she said. As she was driving, she made a sharp turn. Some of Ethan's cheerios spilled onto the floor.

"Here we go," Devonte said. He may not have remembered everything, but he remembered the outcome of this catastrophe. The green Tahoe screeched to a stop at a red light.

"You're going to have to pick all of that up, young man," she exclaimed furiously. Ethan had a sheepish look on his face.

"And don't try the cow eyes. That won't work on me," she retorted. It was true. No matter how cute Ethan tried to look, it didn't change her mind.

"His efforts are futile against her. She has parenting skills of a veteran," Devonte thought. Suddenly, a brief memory flashed across his mind. Devonte was on a soccer field. He saw the shadowy figure similar to the one from his other flashback. He was standing in the distance next to a figure that looked like his mother. It appeared to be a male. There were also two other figures standing next to them. Someone kicked a soccer ball and scored a goal. A referee blew a whistle, and he snapped out of his flashback.

"You alright, son?" Devonte's mother asked. They had already made it to church. Ethan got out of the car and was still munching on cheerios.

"Yeah, just tired is all," Devonte responded. His mother shrugged her shoulders and got out of the Tahoe. Ethan, Devonte, and his mother made their way towards the sanctuary with immense ease and swiftness. They entered and stayed for the whole service. After church, they had lunch with the congregation. They ate ribs, yams, green beans, and bowls of mac and cheese. They also drank ginger ale mixed with a strawberry flavor. This beverage is often otherwise known as Shirley Temple as Ethan took a sip of it, a vast scowl formed on his face. Devonte, on the other hand, very much enjoyed the sugary combination. Their mother would rather have water. The sugary mix was not her forte either.

They then shook hands with a few friends and family in the reception hall. They met a new member who wore a patterned Hawaiian shirt and some cargo shorts. Prudently, the man took some pictures for Facebook. After that, they went home.

CHAPTER 10

Metal Detectors

The day of the trip arrived. Devonte was concerned about the new Oze cable box they installed the other day. Each time he walked by, it seemed to come alive with the flash of its small green light. The channels on it were not much different from the channels on their old cable box. It was as if they connected it for another reason. Devonte stared at it. The cable box sat motionless yet somehow seemed alive. It was forever watching him...As if it were a ghost from the past. He did not understand why, but it felt like the cable box was surveying him, keeping track of his daily movements.

"Maybe it's just me," Devonte supposed. "Well, today is the day, so I better get right to it." He checked his phone. Monique sent a message in the group chat. It read: 1738 Melbourne Drive, 10 a.m. He responded with a text back of two thumbs up emojis then put his phone back in his pocket. He walked upstairs for a quick sweep of his room. He double-checked his desk drawers to make sure he didn't leave anything he might need on the trip.

The amethyst relic was secured safely in his left pocket. Devonte had packed vacation clothes and spare towels into a dark leather magenta suitcase. He also packed some travel dental floss, his navy-blue toothbrush, shower sandals, and shower soap. As he was packing, he looked out the window. A yellow American Goldfinch was perched on a tree. It was blissfully singing a cheerful song.

"Fascinating creature," he thought. He took a picture of the Goldfinch with his camera. Its bright yellow plumage signaled like a beacon amongst the green tree branches. It looked at Devonte then gracefully flew away. He carried his suitcase and grey backpack down the stairs and back towards the living room. Ethan was now watching a documentary about penguins for kids. Like clockwork, the Oze box blinked its green LED light. His mother, also downstairs, was now cutting a pineapple into small slices.

"Don't forget to save your scholarship money. Don't spend it all," she reminded him. Devonte nodded and said, alright.

"And have fun," his mother smiled as she hugged him. She was glad that he had made new friends and was going on an adventure with them. He then checked his quartz watch. The time was now 9:00 a.m. He remembered that they had to meet up at her lab in an hour. With his suitcase in hand, he walked towards Ethan.

"Hey, little man. I'm going to be going away for a while. This weekend I'm going on a three-day vacation with some friends." Ethan looked up at Devonte.

"Okay big man," he said. Devonte gave Ethan a small hug then walked out the door. Allen was already waiting for him with his Mini Cooper. He was wearing some sunglasses and some khaki cargo shorts.

"Yo, we should hustle over there. We said we wanted to be early, remember?" Allen chuckled. Devonte hopped in, and they headed off towards Monique's lab. As they arrived, Ivan was already there. He had taken an uber and wanted to arrive early as well. In his possession was a vintage wooden Winnsboro travel briefcase.

"Cheers, mates. This trip should be fun," he said with optimism. Ivan, Devonte, and Allen were now standing outside of Monique's lab. His Terrier fluffy was nowhere to be found, which meant he had found a suitable sitter. Monique's lavender Lexus rolled around a corner and parked near their vehicles with grandeur and splendor. She hopped out of the car, wearing an army green trench coat. Her dreadlocks were flowing with the wind.

"Well then, I suppose we'd better get going," she said securely. In her hand was the tracking device. It was pointing towards Christmas Island. "The panflute is there, supposedly," Monique said.

"We'll find it," Devonte said boldly. He was sure that the Silver Panflute was there. He had a feeling in his heart. Ivan placed his wooden briefcase in the back of Allen's Mini

Cooper. It sat next to Allen's crimson red suitcase. In the back trunk, there were also some shoeboxes. The sizes ranged from 9.5 all the way up to 12.

"Just have to deliver a few orders when we get back," Allen stated. This practice of being overprepared has aided Allen many times. It has allowed him to stay ready whenever an opportunity presented itself. Allen took out a few folded receipts that he had printed out at home and put them in their respective shoe boxes.

"I just got off the phone with my airplane guy again. He says he can get us a flight to Jakarta. We will have to take a transfer flight to get to Christmas Island from there," she said. Monique then put the airport's address into her GPS. Her lavender Lexus pulled off. Allen, Iven, and Devonte followed her in the Mini Cooper.

Finally, they had arrived at the airport. Monique parked her lavender Lexus, and Allen parked his Mini Cooper. They parked in a parking deck. Devonte looked up at a sign nearby. This was an area dedicated to long term extended-stay parking.

"What an interesting idea," Devonte thought. Families were rushing about, registering their vehicles, and paying for rentals. Many of them had plans to enjoy a long, 2-week vacation. Their hondas and corollas would be waiting for them in their absence. Some time away would not deteriorate them too much. Devonte looked with eyes of wonder and absorbed it all. Around them, they saw rental cars of all types of models. Muscle cars, Sports cars, SUVs, and trucks were all lined up ready for use. After picking the lot closest to the entrance, Monique registered their vehicles for the trip.

"I managed to get our airfare at a 50% discount through my plane guy," Monique grinned.

"That's awesome," Allen applauded. He then hauled his suitcase in the parking deck towards the main airport building. Monique, Ivan, and Devonte followed. They went up an escalator and moved towards the baggage check-in area. There was a line of people waiting to get their luggage approved. After standing in line for about twenty minutes, it was their turn. Devonte presented his dark leather magenta suitcase. Ivan gave an attendant his vintage wooden Winnsboro travel briefcase. Allen contributed his small crimson red suitcase. Monique's slightly large satchel was cleared as a carry-on bag. They all paid their travel fees and then walked into another line area.

After getting through a long line with metal detectors, they found themselves in the airport terminal. Families were stopping by fast-food restaurants, within the airport, buying lunch. Business people in sports coats were walking with phones held close to their ears. Photographers were snapping photographs for future airline advertisements. Students were traveling for study abroad trips, and journalists traveling to assigned locations. It was a lively scene.

"So, this is what an airport looks like?" Devonte accidentally said aloud. Even though he had been to the Caribbean, he did not remember his trip. He was fascinated by this environment. It was quite different from the other sights he had seen today.

CHAPTER 11

Transfer Flight

"Yeah. Don't wander off, it is easy to get lost in places like these," Allen warned. He knew that it was dangerous for Devonte to travel alone in an area like this in his current condition.

"Alright. I'll be sure to stay close," Devonte responded. They walked towards a room filled with chairs and large windows. Outside of the windows, Devonte could see large, metallic machines and pumps connected to airplanes. After reading their tickets, they found the area they were supposed to be seated in. The gatekeeper was waiting for them. They checked in, then sat down across from a man wearing a grey scarf. He was swiping through a news article on his tablet.

"Maybe we should use the restroom before we get on the plane," Allen suggested.

"Already went," Devonte said.

"Well, I have to go," Allen said as he rushed in search of the nearest restroom.

"I'm starving. I'm going to grab a bite to eat," Ivan said. He then went in search of the nearest burrito restaurant. Monique and Devonte were left alone.

"So, you're telling me we're related?" Devonte asked.

"Yep. Somewhere down along the line, you are my long-lost cousin," Monique said. "I researched it some time ago on my search for the relics." Devonte then gave a slight nod of approval.

"The airport terminal is so busy, I don't remember ever seeing anything like it," Devonte said.

"You think this is busy? Just wait until you visit New York," Monique laughed. She was well-traveled. Devonte took out his phone and typed New York in on the browser. Several images appeared of Times Square and different holiday celebrations. He then noticed a similar image to one of his flashbacks.

"New York...I must have already been there before," Devonte thought. He saw a similar digital countdown clock to the one from his flashback. The site read: " New Year's Celebration, New York: Times square ball drop." A few minutes passed, and Allen and Ivan returned. Ivan was holding a thick burrito wrapped in an aluminum foil. Allen had bought a big pack of fruit snacks.

"Flight 99 boarding soon," the overhead intercom announced. The group looked ahead and saw a few passengers begin entering the aerobridge. Above the entrance was a digital sign that read, "Now boarding flight 99."

"Do you think I have time to buy a tote?" Monique asked. She was looking at a travel bag shop with small canvas tote bags.

"You probably won't have time, realistically," Devonte said. He was looking at the passenger boarding bridge. People were now boarding the plane with hushed but evident haste.

"Flight 99 boarding soon," the overhead intercom repeated. A small family with matching tie-dye t-shirts boarded the plane.

"Yeah, you're probably right. It is probably best to stay focused," Monique agreed.

"Encraty," Devonte said firmly.

"Encraty," Monique smiled and shook her head. They boarded the plane and sat in rows next to each other based on their designated ticket seating. Allen and Devonte got window seats. There was a flight attendant up front who taught the passengers how to use airbags in case of an emergency. After they were instructed how to follow the basic safety procedures, everyone was told to buckle their seatbelts. The plane disconnected from the air gate.

"This is the best part," Allen grinned. The plane began moving. It took a slight turn and moved towards the airstrip. After building some speed and momentum, it took off. The aircraft ascended high into the air. They were kilometers above the ground within a few minutes.

"Woah, what a view," Devonte said. He didn't remember ever seeing such.

"I'm going to take a nap so we can get their faster," Allen said. He then drifted off into a deep sleep. The other passengers around him had the same idea. Ivan was reading a plane magazine that he got from the pocket in front of his seat.

"I don't fancy you'd like one too?" Ivan offered a different magazine to Devonte.

"Sure," Devonte accepted. It was a national geographic magazine with a lion on the front cover. Suddenly, a brief memory flashed across his mind. Once again, this memory felt different from the others.

He was standing on a prairie. There were trees scattered on the grassland that was thin at the stem but with branches spread out wide.

"Strange looking trees," Devonte said, curiously. He then saw three tall human figures in the distance wearing large masks. The figures appeared to be male. He couldn't make out what they were standing around, but it looked important. In the distance, he caught sight of two lions steadily approaching the figures.

"Oh no. I hope they get out of there safely," Devonte thought. Just then, a fourth figure appeared. He looked strong. The others began to notice the lions and put their hands on their heads, in dismay. The fourth figure picked up a weapon that looked like a javelin. He threw it when the lions were within range...One hit, one kill. The other ran off. He then joined the other three. In the middle of them was a gazelle, the prize of a hunt. Devonte then snapped out of his flashback. He looked out the window. They had already landed.

"Yo, Come on!" Allen said as he woke Devonte up. It was as if he was the one who had decided to take a nap. They hurried out the plane to find Monique and Ivan already in the airport terminal.

"Alright let's see," Monique said as she was looking through text messages on her phone. "My plane guy says that the flight to Christmas Island is a smaller, non-commercial flight." Ivan, Devonte, and Allen looked at each other in disbelief.

"You're saying we have to get on another plane?" Ivan complained.

"Yes," This is the only flight to Christmas Island, I could get in this time frame," Monique affirmed. She continued to search through her phone.

CHAPTER 12

Baggage Claim

Finally, she found the text message from her plane guy with the location of the private hanger.

"This plane better not have chickens on it," Allen groaned. They exited the boarding area and walked towards the baggage claim area. They saw bags with stripes on them, bags made of metal, and even luxury bags based on modern minimalist designs. Allen grabbed his red suitcase. Monique took her large satchel. Devonte found his dark magenta suitcase. Ivan picked up his vintage travel briefcase. They began walking towards a revolving metal door. As they went out, one by one, the door swung open in progression, like clockwork. Their luggage trailed behind them. Monique was leading the way. The text on her phone told her to go to hanger number 42. They walked along the airstrip and looked at the hanger numbers.

"45...44...43...Aha, 42," Monique exclaimed. The hanger was open. Allen Ivan, Devonte, and Monique stormed in. Inside the hanger was a small red seaplane. Standing next to it was a young red-haired woman.

"So, you're the ones that Walter sent? What a curious crew," the woman sighed.

"I'm Savannah. Welcome to my hanger," She then friendly said. She walked over towards the group to shake hands and greet them. "This here is the Red Canary, the fastest plane on this side of the Mississippi," she declared.

"Nice plane," Allen said. He was fascinated by the skis attached to the bottom of it.

"These allow this bad boy to take off and land on bodies of water," Savannah boasted.

"I wonder if it can drive on water," Devonte thought. The idea of a water plane seemed cool. Ivan Stepped out from around the back.

"Well, what are we waiting for? Let's head to Christmas Island," Ivan said eagerly. The group piled their luggage into the small seaplane.

"You all can sit in the back. I got my pilot's license last year and can help out up here," Monique said, She sat in the cockpit beside Savannah and put on the pilot headphones that were in the seat. The two pulled a throttle and switched some knobs. The plane slowly began to move out of the hanger. After the aircraft was fully out of the hanger, Savannah turned off the engine. Savannah tapped on a key-encrypted remote outside. The hanger began to close. She then got back into the plane.

They started up the plane again, and it slowly began to move towards the runway.

"Here we go," Allen uttered. The plane began to drive full throttle. The plane then took off. It steadily climbed high into the air. Ivan decided to take a nap this time around. He was tired from the last light and did not feel like staying awake for another one. Devonte and Allen sat in enthusiasm. After the tricky process of the airport, they were finally on their way to Christmas Island. As they neared the island, the ride became slightly bumpy. The wind was blowing hard on the small red seaplane. It's metal was not built to experience such turbulence.

"Woah. It looks like we have some high winds here," Monique gasped. She began steering the plane more forcefully to stay on course.

"Maybe we should head back," Savannah advised.

"No, we're almost there might as well go ahead and follow through with it," Devonte said. The two in the cockpit shrugged and continued to fly in the high winds. Just then, Allen spotted an island.

"Yo, look. There it is," he exclaimed. From a bird's eye view, the island itself looked like a dog-faced to the right. Ivan woke up.

"Well that's a beauty," Ivan cackled. On the island, they saw a faint red hue, but they couldn't make out what was making the color.

"I'm going to circle the island then land near one of those beaches," Savannah said. She did what she said she would. Savannah piloted the plane to a beach clearing and initiated her landing gear.

"Let's be sure not to hurt any animals. Be careful," Monique warned.

"We won't. I'm the best pilot around," Savannah said. She then landed the plane softly onto the water.

"Ladies and gentlemen...experience the absolute wonder of this plane. The Canary can land on absolutely any barren landscape or rustling waterscape known to man or...woman," Savannah said. She then guided the landing gear to kiss the ocean softly. Her seaplane coasted for a moment on the ocean's blustery waves. It's propellers then hushed their whirling, and the seaplane came to a complete stop.

Christmas Island was a sight to behold. The seafoam from ocean waves drifted and flowed with the direction of the tides. Out of the plane's window, they could see mountain ridges covered with vegetation in the distance. Palm trees where adorned and scattered throughout the beach. A small group of sea birds was using the island as a resting area for their long migration. As they were watching this, the waves pushed and pulled against the seaplane.

"So, the silver panflute is supposed to be here? How in the world are we going to find it?" Allen complained.

"My tracker is never wrong. If it says it's here, then it must be around here somewhere," Monique declared. Devonte looked up. Dark clouds were forming.

"Well whatever we do, we better do it quickly. It looks like it's about to rain," Devonte proposed.

"That's tough," Allen said. He had only packed a small track jacket.

"It happens, mate. That's why I always bring my fleece windbreaker, to battle inclement weather," Ivan said. He was used to weather changing dramatically on trips. Just then, Monique took a small spyglass from out of her satchel and looked at something in the distance.

"There are also more pressing matters than inclement weather. Look over there in the distance!" Monique called out. There was a small yacht, two klicks out from where they were.

"We are not alone," she said in a hushed tone.

"Let me see," Devonte said, interested in what she was seeing. He to his eye and focused its lenses until it was crystal clear. On the boat was a man with a thick mustache wearing a grey collar shirt with matching grey gloves. It was the man from the Solstice Festival.

CHAPTER 13

Crab Rave

Allen, Devonte, Ivan, Monique, and Savannah got out of the plane and wafted towards the shore. As they walked, Devonte looked back. The yacht had turned towards their direction and stopped sailing.

"Do you recognize that man, Devonte?" Monique questioned.

"That's the same mustached man from the festival. When he came near, I could feel the Amethyst pulsing in my pocket and glowing," Devonte affirmed.

"That's not good. It never does that without reason," Monique said, now anxious.

"Let's get this over with," Allen said. "Those guys seem like bad news. They must be looking for the panflute too."

"We don't want the amulet to fall into bad hands," Ivan said.

"I'll wait and keep an eye on the Canary," Savannah said warily. She was watching the yacht intensely.

"Aha, I've got something," Monique said as her tracking device started beeping. "We should follow this signal. It will lead us in closer proximity to the Silver Panflute," she said. They walked away from the beach and into the island forest. Skinks and geckos were springing out from under tree branches and tree roots. The trees were towering above, giving off the feeling of an older brother or helicopter parent hovering above their shoulders.

Suddenly, as they were walking, they came upon a clearing with some rocks. A peculiar sight was there waiting for them.

"Yo…That's mad crazy. Look," Allen exclaimed. On the rocks was a sea of red crabs scurrying and rushing from one place to the next.

"Look at all of them," Ivan said enthusiastically.

Devonte took the waterproof camera out of his grey backpack and snapped some quick photographs. The crabs were moving frenetically and wildly. Some of them were moving in the same motions, almost as if they were in sync. It was a crab rave.

"Ivan walked towards one of the crabs. Hey little fella. You having fun?" Ivan said. The crab snapped at him and scurried away frantically.

"Animals really just do not like you," Allen laughed. "You must have let a goldfish die or something."

"Funny you should mention that," Ivan said with a sheepish look on his face. That did happen.

They went past and clearing and continued walking into the

forest. As they went deeper into the forest, Devonte took out the amethyst. He noticed the amethyst relic slightly flickering on and off.

"We're getting closer," Monique said. Her tracking device was flashing and beeping zealously. As she was scanning, she walked with strides of great determination and willpower. The tracking device was pointing fervently. It took them over large forest hills and through deep valleys.

"Did you know that this Christmas Island has inhabitants from over 50 different species?" Monique said with zeal and enthusiasm. Ivan intently listened as she went on and one spewing these facts with curiosity and interest. Devonte was also intrigued. They continued walking and came upon a small ravine. Just then, a brief memory flashed across his mind.

He was in a high school basketball gym. It was a school basketball game. The score was 64 to 63, Devonte's team was down. There were only 4 seconds on the clock. People were sitting on the edge of their seats watching in eagerness and anticipation. A wingman inbounded the ball. They made two quick passes. Devonte now had it. The clock ticked down to milliseconds. He cleared space and released a routine shot with flawless form, almost unconsciously. The crowd was dead silent as the ball flew into the air. The buzzer sounded...Swish.

The once inanimate crowd now roared. The entire team ran onto the court in victory and celebration. Classmates were waving blue towels. His coach looked from afar and nodded. Teachers were smiling in disbelief and astonishment. Some players on the opposing team were subtly sniffing, and tears began to form. A shadowy figure similar to the one's in his other memories viewed from a distance.

Devonte snapped out of his flashback. Unexpectedly, he took a few steps backward. He then began a full sprint towards the ravine jumping across effortlessly.

"Woah, now those are some hops," Ivan complimented.

"Just like in the old days," Allen said.

"Yeah, I just remembered how we won the championship," Devonte attested. The rest of them walked down into and out of the ravine. They continued walking deeper into the island forest. Allen, Monique, Devonte, and Ivan leaped over rocks and fallen tree branches. It was a good workout.

Monique's tracking device took them a sharp right turn. They followed the path they were suggested. Devonte saw a brown butterfly with brown spots.

"Nice," Devonte said, as he snapped a photograph. Soon they came upon another clearing in the forest. They approached the base of a relatively large hill. Near the bottom of the large hill, was the mouth of a sizeable cave.

"Wait...we have to go in...there?" Allen protested. He was very reluctant to venture into an unknown cave without first having information on it.

"But of course. These are the caves of Christmas island," Monique said as she pulled a lighter out of her satchel. "I expected the panflute to be in a cave. I predicted it to be either that or buried with treasure."

"Well, shiver me timbers. That would be better than this," Allen said sarcastically. He really did not want to go into the cave. "Maybe we can circle back and check."

"The tracking device points in there. We must retrieve it," Monique declared. She then took a lighter from out of her satchel. With two strikes, she created a small bonfire in a nearby patch of grass. There was also a short bush nearby. She grabbed four short sticks from the bush and attached some fire fuel using some nearby vines. After momentarily dipping the sticks into the bonfire, they now had torches. Devonte grabbed a torch and led the way inside.

CHAPTER 14

Christmas Caves

The cave was cold... really cold. Water was dripping from the cave stalactites into small puddles. Devonte looked at his reflection in the puddles. He was a dark, tall young man with jet black hair in medium twists.

Monique's torch flickered brightly against the cave's moist walls. Devonte's torch burned brightly against the walls. Ivan's torch was slightly larger than the other torches. Allen clung to his torch tightly.

"A-Are those...BATS?" Allen yelped. He was now giving his full attention to the ceiling of the cave.

"There hasn't been a confirmed sighting of the Christmas Island pipistrelle since 2009," Monique sighed.

"The pipi-what?" Allen asked with a perplexed look on his face.

"The Christmas Island pipistrelle. That's the scientific name for this species of vesper bat only found on Christmas Island, Australia," Monique clarified. "It is now pronounced to be extinct."

"Well, that's a relief," Ivan responded. He shined his flashlight at the bat-like shapes on the ceiling. They turned out to be shadows.

"Not for the bats," Monique retorted. "The increase in civilization and tourist activity has had a major effect on the environment. Many people have come to view the crab migrations, I suppose," Monique said as she paced around. After coming to a stop, she took out a note pad from her satchel and started scribbling down some notes. "Nevertheless, I believe all of this has made it difficult for species such as the Christmas Island pipistrelle to survive."

"Oh. That's tough," Allen replied.

"Having your home invaded, used, and then exploited to acquire profit...that sounds terrible," Ivan said.

"It is," Monique said with a frown. "I wish we could bring back the bats and rehabilitate them into an environment better than the one that was taken from them. It really is a shame. You can't bring back the dead."

"They deserve that and more," Ivan said. He had converted his previous fear of the bats into sympathy. He now began to feel bad for them. The bats did not ask to have their home infiltrated or occupied.

"We should keep moving," Devonte testified. They continued on deeper into the cave. Fairly large cobwebs were stuck on the cave walls. Their creators were long gone. The passage of age had taken its toll.

"I wonder who could have made those," Ivan said sarcastically.

"S-Spiders! This place gives me the creeps," Allen cried. A shiver went down his spine as he said this. They continued walking. As they marched on, they noticed that the walls were starting to radiate a faint silver glow. The light was emitted from a source much deeper in the cave. Ivan, Allen, Devonte, and Monique were closing in on the location depicted on the tracking device. Although they could not see it physically, they could feel a different atmosphere around this section of the cave. The air became more arid and tense.

It was hidden and, therefore, undisturbed. It felt as if this part of the cave was more ancient. It was dead silent. Only movement and activity coming from cave salamanders could be heard. They were patiently waiting for signs of their next meal. These crawling amphibians ate bugs and small vermin that resided along the cave's floor. They were fed often and regularly had their fill, snacking on beetles, ants, and cave spiders. Some salamanders looked up at Allen, Devonte, Monique, and Ivan in wonder. The newcomers looked as if they were alien visitors from another planet. They seemed lost and not accustomed to the rules and life of a cave dweller. Eventually, the salamanders disregarded them and continued to scurry and rush about.

Suddenly a big tan beetle flew through the cave opening that they came from. It was flying in a zigzag motion.

"That's disgusting," Devonte said. He was not very fond of winged insects, especially beetles.

"That is the notorious Christmas Beetle. They are a special type of scarab beetle that resides on this island," Monique responded. "Eucalyptus leaves make up their primary diet." Sounds of its fluttering wings echoed through the cave as it escaped into the sunlight. The updraft of the cave's acoustics amplified the sounds until they merged into a convergence of echoes and hums. If there were any bats left alive, they would have heard the cries through echolocation and made a quick meal of them. A general conclusion to make would be to assume that the beetles were sending matting calls towards one another and were looking forward to procreating.

After this beetle encounter, they turned a cave corner. This section of the cave was different from the rest. There were four streams of light pouring into the cave thorough glassy, translucent, half-crystalline, half-mineral windows. The light streams were exposing small clusters of dust floating in the room.

"We're here," Monique declared. She pulled out the map from her pocket and got ready to cross the panflute off the list.

"That should about do it for our trip," Monique said with a sigh of relief. However, Allen, Devonte, and Ivan looked up with a frown.

"Uh, Monique," Allen said shakily.

"I think you should take a look at this," Devonte said decisively. Monique stopped scribbling notes about endangered island species and calmly put her notepad away. She looked up and then also had a frown. In the middle of the four streams of light, was not the Silver Panflute.

"Oh no," Monique cried. "There has been a mistake." Allen, Ivan, and Devonte looked at Monique.

"What do you mean there's been a mistake?" Devonte asked. They didn't pay for long term airport parking and fly on two planes to follow her all the way to the island, just to be let down.

"It's not here," Ivan said astutely. As he said this, his words reverberated and echoed against the cave walls. He was correct. Their eyes glanced about the expanse of this special section of the cave. There was no silver panflute in sight.

CHAPTER 15

Abandoned Blade

"My tracking device seldom has an error. This is unbelievable," Monique sighed. "It was set for the Silver Panflute, but instead it is pointed for the renowned sword, Crocea Mors. A foreign radio frequency must have disrupted the device from its proper channel while we were on the plane." They peeped into the cave opening with the faint silver glow. There was an engraved sword with an elaborate; handcrafted handle stuck in a bronze shield.

"A blade once used by Julius Caesar, Crocea Mors, otherwise known as the "Yellow Death", was a sword of Julius Caesar," Monique continued. "It was said to be hand-fashioned by Vulcan himself. It was a gift to Aeneas from the Roman goddess Venus. Caesar somehow obtained it and carried it with him until he battled the British prince, Nennius. He lost the sword when it became lodged into Nennius' shield."

"That's mad crazy. I thought we came here to find the Silver Panflute," Allen sighed. "Is the sword just as special?" He asked.

"Unfortunately, I'm not sure. From my sources, I hear it's just a regular sword, but it looks cool," Monique said optimistically.

"Well, we didn't come all this way to leave empty-handed," Devonte said sensibly. "Stand back."
Allen, Ivan, and Monique stood back. He pulled out the amethyst relic. It was giving off a faint ominous violet glow.

"Here we go, let's see what you can do," Devonte thought to himself. He aimed it at the sword stuck in the shield.

"Let's hope that thing doesn't blow us up," Allen said, although he wanted it to activate as well.

"Be careful not to break it," Monique advised. "That may not be a relic as useful as the others. However, it is still a relic, nonetheless."

"I'll keep a note of that," Devonte said, as he continued aiming the amethyst at Crocea Mors. His hand was shaking steadily. The amethyst began to pulse again. This time, it was pulsating in harmonic rhythm. Devonte, still aiming for the sword that was stuck in the shield, hit the gemstone a little with his hand. It immediately shot out an ultraviolet ray of light and cracked the shield in two. They stood back in astonishment. The Crocea Mors was gleaming with great craftsmanship and ardor. Despite the fact that it had been abandoned and moved to this location by fate. Devonte picked the sword up and admired it for a second. It had dust in its ridges and probably could use a sharpening. However, it was a great find.

"This will help us in our journey for sure," Allen said. "Remember those cobwebs? I say we kill whatever monstrosity made those whenever we get the chance."

"It's not that simple," Monique said. "First, we have to determine whether or not that species is on the endangered list. It would be a shame to cause another animal species to go extinct on this biodiverse island." Apparently, Monique was also an environmentalist. Suddenly, Devonte remembered that she was known for her elaborate conservationist schemes for protecting the earth and its wildlife inhabitants.

"Well that explains a lot," Devonte said. Monique had spent years studying historical artifacts, but she also had knowledge of the animal kingdom. She had looked over encyclopedias containing facts about many different Insects, birds, mammals, and even fish. Her notepad had a special section dedicated specifically to charting endangered species and rare animals.

"The elusive Snow Leopard is on the top of my list of endangered species," Monique said in a hushed tone. "It is a rare magnificent creature in the south and central Asia, that only shows itself when it wants to be seen."

"Snow Leopard?" Allen said heartily. He had never seen a snow leopard before, let alone a regular leopard.

"Yes, indeed. Snow Leopards are among the rarest of endangered species ranked relatively high on the list," Monique mentioned. As she was talking, Devonte swung the abandoned blade around. It made woosh sounds as it sliced through the air. He had never used a sword before and was very interested in what it could cut through.

Suddenly, Ivan shinned his flashlight towards the way back where they came.

"Come on, mates. We should regroup and maybe look for the Silver Panflute, another time at another place," Ivan said. Devonte was cutting through the air as if his hand were an airplane rotor. The metal swish sound slightly was felt as the air was disturbed and altered.

"Alright. I'll bring the sword with me," said Devonte. They walked towards the exit of the cave. They walked out of the ancient chamber with the four streams of light pouring in. They walked past the active cave salamanders moving hastily about. They walked towards the area of the cave where Allen thought bats were watching them. Allen held up his torch towards the cave ceiling. There was still not a single bat in sight.

"Maybe we should double-check the tracking device every once in a while, so this doesn't happen again," Allen suggested.

"Good idea, mate," Ivan agreed. Ivan was walking with a spring in his step. He missed his Terrier. He was probably off somewhere, causing trouble or planning another escape attempt.

"I will certainly do that here on out. There is much to take into consideration. A turbulent flight? No...wait I knew the location before that," Monique said as she paused, and deep thoughts entered her cerebellum. "Aha! It would have had to be before we ventured out from my lab on Saturday," She exclaimed. Suddenly she frowned. Monique had come to a unique realization. She knew that her tracking device had not moved off course by mere happenstance or coincidence. Someone had deliberately arranged for them to reach this location. She also knew that whoever had led them astray was probably nearby.

"We should be cautious. Here, Allen, you take the sword," Devonte said as he handed over the sword. Allen clutched the sword fervently with both hands.

"I get to keep this?" Allen said. Devonte took out the amethyst relic. It was now glowing.

"You all stay behind, we'll go first," he said. Finally, they exited the entrance of the cave. As Monique had predicted, there was a man in a bowler hat waiting for them.

CHAPTER 16

Winter's Edge

"Excellent work, I really ought to thank you," The man in the bowler hat said.

"W-Who are you?" Allen said frightfully.

"Who am I? Why, I am Mr. McFlynn, master of the seven provinces, seeker of the Sichuan, keeper of the sacred scrolls. Surely, you've heard of me?" he went on.

"Doesn't ring a bell," Devonte opposed.

"Nevertheless, you've retrieved something very special that belongs to me," Mr. McFlynn said irately.

"What?" Ivan inquired inquisitively.

"Crocea Mors, a blade of conquest and triumph. Left here by forgotten predecessors, fate destined it to return back into the hands of a conqueror," said Mr. McFlynn.

"We came all this way to get the bloody thing, and it turns out to be a hoax, a swindle at that? Such an unfortunate turn of events," Ivan sighed.

"And look at that, you've even freed it from that obnoxious shield encasement for me," Mr. McFlynn added.

"Listen, we don't want any trouble," Monique proposed.

"Neither do I. I am the rightful ruler of the relics. So, if you'll be so kind, I'll be taking it back with me," Mr. McFlynn snarled.

The amethyst was shining brighter than before.

"We found it fair and square," Devonte declared. He was determined to go home with the sword.

"Then you leave me no choice," Mr. McFlynn growled. He took out an old-fashioned bronze music box from out of his pocket. As he opened it, Monique caught sight of a tiny ballerina inside. An ominous tune played. All of a sudden more butterflies with brown spots poured out of the cave.
They surrounded Monique, Allen, Ivan, and Devonte.

"Quick, use the relic!" Monique cried. Devonte aimed the relic to the left, hoping to make a break for it. The amethyst started to pulse. It was pulsing in a harmonic rhythm again.

"Do it now!" Allen yelled. A circle of butterflies was forming around them. It was getting smaller.

"Hurry mate, these nasty bugs are biting," Ivan added. The butterflies began to nip and gnaw at them. Then with a quick flash of his ultraviolet light, Devonte created a path for them to escape. They followed closely behind him and sprinted into the forest.

"You can run, but you can't hide! I will find those relics if it's the last thing I do!" Mr. McFlynn hollered. They didn't look back. Allen caught up to Devonte and began using the sword to cut vines and small branches blocking their path.

"This sword is sharp," Allen said ardently. The Crocea Mors was a blade of great integrity. It greatly lived up to its expectations. It was as sharp as winter's edge. Allen began to cut and slice through the stubborn entangled vines and branches unconsciously. He did so without the feel of the blade or the vegetation in their path in which it removed.

"Woah, that is sharp," Ivan concurred. Ivan agreed with Monique's earlier assumption. The Crocea Mors was special, after all. Now he was eager to find out what the other more important relics could do. After they were far enough, their sprint had turned into a light jog.

"Let's keep moving. We don't want to run into that Mr. McFlynn gentleman again anytime soon," Devonte suggested. They continued jogging. Monique checked her tracking device. It was still pointed towards the Silver Panflute. She was now even more cautious.

"Who was that??" Allen exclaimed. "That guy almost took us out with a music box."

"The real question is, how did he manage to control those butterflies like that?" Ivan asked. "Incredible. Scary, but Incredible."

"I wonder how they managed to do that," Monique said aloud. "I definitely need to make some major upgrades once I return to the lab," she said.

"Most definitely," Allen agreed. "Even though this sword is cool, we did not have to go in that creepy cave." Their light jogging now calmed down to a slower pace.

"It wasn't so bad as long as we found a relic. It may not be the fanciest relic, but it will do for now," Ivan claimed.

"He's right," Devonte said. "We should be thankful that we did find one out of the few relics out there."

"There is that optimism that I'm used to," Monique mentioned happily. Devonte had a mystified look on his face. Just then, a brief memory flashed across his mind.

He was sitting in a Doctor's office...no it was a Dentist's office. His little brother Ethan was with him. He looked younger and was seated beside him. There was a fairly large fish tank nearby with aesthetic angelfish, colorful clownfish, and an energetic tiger barb.

"Will it hurt?" Ethan asked, looking at Devonte. Just then, before he could respond, a shadow of himself appeared in front of him.

"Not at all. The dentist is just going to clean your teeth," Devonte's shadow said.

"What about that big x-ray machine," Ethan said. He looked and pointed towards a room with a large machine in it.

"Oh, that? That's just a fancy machine for getting a closer look at your teeth. They have to check and see if you have cavities, and then they clean," Devonte's shadow reassured.

"Ok," Ethan said sheepishly. "You're so brave. When I grow up, I want to be just like you," he added. He snapped out of his flashback.

"Yo, you good? You stared off into space again," Allen said.

"Yeah, I'm alright," Devonte replied. They entered the forest clearing. There were no red crabs this time. Instead, there was a sight even more peculiar.

CHAPTER 17

Shimmering Leaves

As they stood in the clearing, Devonte, Monique, Ivan, and Allen saw a marvelous sight. The leaves around them were encased with a reflective glow. It was almost as if the leaves had chlorophyll made of gemstones.

"Woah, that's something you don't see every day," Devonte said. The leaves were shimmering and shining as if they were prisms about to burst with all different hues of light.

"That's interesting. Weren't the leaves just normal a moment ago?" Ivan alleged.

"Fascinating," Monique agreed. She pulled out her notepad again and started taking more notes. As the leaves were swaying in the wind, they began to change colors compulsively. It was an opalescent sight of great majesty and wonder. Devonte took his waterproof camera from out of his grey backpack and started taking pictures.

"Have to capture the moment," he said. Devonte then proceeded to take snapshots of the trees surrounding the clearing. They stood tall, towering above them with a hint of distinction in their vicinity.

"It does that too? That's mad crazy," Allen said. Suddenly they all looked back at Allen. He was holding the sword up pointed towards the heavens. He looked almost as if he were a legendary warrior from a past time.

"How are you doing that?" Devonte inquired. The sword also had light shimmering around it.

"I'm not sure, but it's pretty cool," Allen said enthusiastically. Ivan was gazing at the Crocea Mors as well. It was pulsing and flashing in an ardent light.

"That energy looks dangerous. You should probably save that for later," Monique said perceptively. A saddened look came over Allen's face.

"Oh alright," Allen said gloomily. He began to try to clip the sword onto his belt. The other members of Encraty did not have weapons as big or as sharp. Allen was curious about this sword. He wondered how it was able to warp the environment around them into a colorful reflective paradise. It was not pocket-sized like the other relics. It did not have a distinct color scheme like the others. It was unique. Compared to the other weapons, it was greatly underestimated and misjudged. Nevertheless, it exceeded their expectations as an unforeseen surprise.

The leaves and trees around them looked like they had slightly grown. The vines looked as if they were longer and more entwined. Branches that were once broken had now grown back a little. As he put the sword away, he began to notice a glowing inscription written on the side of the sword.

"Hey guys, look," The sword has something written on it. Ivan, Monique, and Devonte glanced over at the sword. It was pulsing in the same rhythm the amethyst had earlier. It read, "Ad meloria" in cursive letters.

"That must be Latin...Fascinating" Monique said in a hushed voice. She then took down more notes in her notepad.

"I feel like this sword is special after all," Ivan insisted. Allen then sheathed the sword by clipping it onto his belt. As he put the blade away, the leaves stopped shimmering in their luminous light. The leaves returned to their normal shade of green, and the tree trunks became still and tranquil again. A red-tailed tropicbird flew by. It was calling out into the distance with its raspy call. They left the clearing and continued walking. Devonte checked his watch. It was now 5:00 p.m. Allen peaked at Devonte's watch.

"It's the afternoon already?" Allen asked, looking surprised.

"I guess so," Devonte responded. Monique was still deeply pondering the recent events that took place. They began to quicken their pace. They continued walking with hope in their hearts and a spring in their steps. The painted colors of the sunset palette began weaving into the sky.

"What a day," Ivan said. Considering the fact that killer butterflies almost ravaged them, he was thankful that he was still kicking. He was grateful that he had met such brave comrades.

"I agree. Who would've thought we'd get off-track?" Monique said grudgingly.

"It's ok, we found a relic that is just as good," Devonte reassured with a smile. He then proceeded to take out his relic. The amethyst was no longer glowing.

"What if the Silver Panflute isn't all that we hoped it to be?" Allen asked worriedly. "We came all this way looking for it and found this instead." He was now thinking about what would happen if the panflute fell into the wrong hands.

"We'll be fine. We just have to make sure we find it first. The costs of it falling into the wrong hands could be catastrophic," Monique said. Allen was now looking at Devonte and Monique with worry and concern.

"It'll be alright. Just stay calm and positive. We've got to keep our energy up," Devonte said again, encouraging him. This was the same attitude that had won them the championships. Allen looked at Devonte for a second, and his frown faded into a grin.

"Yeah, you're right. We got this," Allen agreed. He then proceeded to think happier thoughts. They would be alright. With some proper searching in the right direction, they would find the Silver Panflute.

"Come on, mates, is that the best we've got? Getting a little thrown off track, won't stop us," Ivan said. He was now also inspired by the encouragement.

"A few positive words can go a long way," Monique said, now looking directly at Devonte. "Keep at it."

"Thanks, I will," Devonte said as he accepted the compliment. He was now certain that encouraging others while they were down was an important part of his character.

"That is a unique thing about you. You are always finding the positive side of things. You definitely have a glass half full perspective," Monique said.

"Well I try," Devonte responded. He put the amethyst relic back into his pocket. All might be revealed in due time if they persisted with a positive outlook.

CHAPTER 18

Pompous Pegasus

Eventually, they made their way back to the beach. They saw the Red Canary. It was still swaying blissfully in the ocean. There was a small rowboat that was docked near the beach with a large stake. It was creating tiny ripples in the water as the wind pushed and pulled it gently. There was no sign of the man with the thick mustache, in the grey collar shirt. Although the yacht was still there, it seemed unoccupied. There was one difference, however. The yacht had a green flag hoisted up with the symbol of a Pegasus on it.

"What do you think that means?" Ivan asked. He wondered if that was an oceanwide universal signal like how a blue flag on the beach means dangerous marine life.

"It was probably just a routine hoist. We should really get moving," Allen said. He was ready to get off of this bizarre island. Besides the sword, it had brought them nothing but trouble in his opinion.

"I wouldn't be surprised if that were their insignia," Monique inferred. She sketched a drawing of the flag on her note pad.

"Maybe it means they are away from the ship," Ivan guessed.

"Don't be ridiculous. Someone had to hoist it. They are probably just below deck waiting for him to return with the blade," Allen deduced.

"It has to mean something," Devonte remarked.

"Woah. Look!" Ivan exclaimed. He was pointing towards the other end of the beach. They glanced over to where he was pointing. The crabs they had seen earlier were headed back into the water. There were tens of thousands of them, each rushing back into the safety of the salty ocean foam. This time, Ivan did not attempt to go greet one. They were rather hostile creatures living free and untamed.

"Most extraordinary," Monique remarked. "As they are immense in number, they are definitely in their migration season. I read an article somewhere that said the Christmas Island red crab is known to travel long journeys to mate and spawn during the autumn months."

The crabs were now bobbing into the water like little red fishing bubble floats. Every time a crab arose to the surface, another one sank into the cool, roaring waters. They were moving with a purpose. Each wave brought more red floats with it, and more sediments of sand thrust up from the crabs before them.

Allen looked at them with eyes of fascination as they took the trek from land to the vast ocean.

"Come on, guys, we have to focus. Playing with the crabs will have to wait. Remember, we have someone chasing us, and we really should be trying to see what that flag means," Devonte said.

"Right," Allen agreed. He was still eager to leave the island regardless of its excitement and wonders. The sunset was now falling fully over the horizon. Red-tailed tropicbirds began to stop chirping. Cicadas, gnats, and moths were buzzing and beginning to call out to each other.

"We should be careful. Don't want to be stuck here after dark. The Canary is our only ticket out of here. We should take it," Monique cautioned. She had no intention of being marooned on Christmas Island.

"Seriously, does anyone have a clue as to what that flag means? That looks like a pegasus with such prestige," Allen asked. The flag was hoisted high and fluttering against the winds of the sea.

"One thing's for sure, it doesn't look like a countries colors mate," Ivan proposed. "Can't say I've seen a flag like that on any map." Being a well-traveled individual, he could recognize flags from most of the countries on this side of the hemisphere.

"Certainly not. There must be a deeper explanation for that strange spectacle," Devonte claimed. Just then, he caught sight of the man with the bowler hat in the distance, catching up to them from the island forest.

"I guess we can figure it out later," Devonte said. He took out his camera and quickly adjusted the focus on the flag. He snapped a photograph and put it away.

"Let's get out of here before they cause any more trouble," Allen said hastily. Devonte and Monique nodded. They wadded in the water and made their way back to the red seaplane.

"Did y'all find what you were looking for?" Savannah beamed as she stepped out of the plane. She had spotted their hearty crew from a mile away.

"Sadly, no. But we found something else," Devonte muttered. Allen drew out the Crocea Mors. It was glistening with a similar glow as before. Suddenly, the red Canary began to shine in the same reflective light that the leaves from earlier had. The propellers began to spin.

"Hurry put that away," Monique said warily. Not knowing it would do this, Allen quickly sheathed it again. The propellers stopped spinning.

"Are you mad? These artifacts are dangerous. You've got to be careful," Ivan exclaimed. Allen put the sword away. Exhausted from their journey, they climbed into the seaplane. Monique sat in the front with Savannah, ready to assist if the flight became turbulent again. She wanted to get back to her lab as soon as possible to analyze and store the artifact.

"Well isn't that something," Savannah said. She was now looking with a perplexed expression on her face.

"What is it? Did I mess up the plane?" Allen asked.

"The fuel gauge is filled to the brim now. Not too shabby," Savannah responded. Thrilled, she fired up the engine, and they flew off.

CHAPTER 19

Industrial Improvement

Savannah, now even more intrigued by the group, decided to fly them all the way home. She landed her seaplane back at Jakarta and picked up a larger plane in a different hanger, owned by her cousin. After sending a text notifying him that she would be borrowing it, they jumped in. The plane's engine started up quickly and efficiently. They swiftly took off and headed home.

They arrived at the airport late in the night, near the debut of dusk. Savannah exchanged numbers with them, and Monique, very kindhearted and welcoming, also added her to the group chat.

"Luckily, I have another cousin I can stay with, who lives here. She's a nice adventurer like me," Savannah said with a laugh. "I'll be around, just let me know when you're ready to go on your next adventure."

"Thanks, much appreciated," Devonte said, showing gratitude. The others also thanked her. She called a ride to where she was staying. After a 5-minute wait, a car came by, and she hopped in. They waved goodbye as she sped off.

"Now, let's see if my Mini Cooper is still here," Allen said doubtfully. Ivan gave him a look.

"Must be his first time traveling," Monique sighed. They walked towards the car rental area. Both the Monique's lavender Lexus and Allen's Mini Cooper were still parked there. Allen let out an exhale of relief.

"Well, at least now I know my mom won't kill me," Allen alleged. Devonte and Ivan looked at him.

"Yeah, you're good," Devonte laughed. They promptly hopped in Allen's Mini Cooper.

"We should rest for a day then regroup. I'm going to add some modifications to my scanner and study the Crocea Mors further," Monique explained. Allen handed her the sword, and she put it in the back of her trunk. Monique then got into her lavender Lexus and drove back to her lab. Ivan, Allen, and Devonte went into the Mini Cooper and back to their homes. They rested for a day like Monique proposed. The following morning the group chat was blowing up. Devonte rolled over and checked his phone. There were 14 new messages from Monique.

"Check this out. You're not going to believe what just happened. It's the Crocea Mors," Monique wrote. Her text messages were jumbled and rushed. "You all should come back to the Lab as soon as possible," she said, finishing her rant. Devonte lazily slipped out of bed. His digital clock sat lifeless and idle, showing the time of 11:30 a.m. He walked into his bathroom to get ready for the day. After getting ready, he threw on day attire, grabbed his grey backpack, and rushed downstairs. A short note was left on the kitchen countertop. It read, "I Took Ethan to a friend's birthday party. Please do the dishes." Devonte quickly cleaned the few dishes in the sink and put them away.

As he did this, he caught sight of the Oze box. It was blinking even more fervently than before. He looked at it and shook his head. He then ate a granola bar and headed out the door. Eager to find out what the sword was doing, Allen was outside waiting for him. His Mini Cooper was poorly parked in Devonte's driveway.

"Yo, did you see the group chat today?" Allen exclaimed as he rushed in with no remorse. Devonte noticed that he was not wearing the clean neon shoes that he had on earlier. He was now wearing some vans with some dirt on them. Devonte motioned for him to get off of the carpet.

"Yeah, I saw it. Looks like she's discovered something interesting about the sword," Devonte replied. "She seemed to be pretty excited."

"Man, we should head over there ASAP," Allen said keenly. He entered in Monique's lab address into the map app on his phone.

"Well, I packed all my stuff, no need to sit around here," Devonte said. He firmly locked the mahogany wood panel door with his bronze key. They then left the house and piled into Allen's Mini Cooper. Ivan was already in the car, waiting for them. They drove off swiftly, blasting some new good music that Allen had discovered. Ivan had on a navy-blue sweater. He chilled in the back. On the way there, they stopped at a gas station. Allen, Ivan, and Devonte hopped out. They went inside. After a brief moment, they went up to the cash register. Ivan placed a large Kit Kat package on the counter. Allen had a variety of coconut flavored candy, and Devonte bought a Skittles bag. After the transactions, Allen paid for the gas and pumped it. They then drove downtown on towards her lab. During the ride, they had an aristocrat's discussion over which candy was the best.

They finally made it to Monique's lab. Devonte checked his watch. It was now noon. Parallel parking with great care, Allen chauffeured them into a decent spot near the steps. Ivan sent a text to the group chat notifying her that they were there. Afterward, they climbed up the steps of the apartment like building. They waited in anticipation for a moment. The door mechanically creaked open, and Monique came out wearing some glasses that seemed new.

"Quick inside. You've got to see this," She said. They walked in behind her, and the door closed shut. Her lab looked like a completely different place. The beakers inside of it looked more sophisticated; the designs of the fortress painting frames looked more refined. She led them back into the violet room. Savannah was sitting inside.

"What is all this? I don't believe all this was here last time we visited," Ivan laughed. He was correct. Last time they were here, her lab was didn't have such complex intricacies.

"It's the sword!" Monique exclaimed. "It has the ability to improve upon anything that you cast its shadow upon." She was now overjoyed with her experimental findings. This relic could put her years ahead in research and industrial improvement.

"Now that's useful," Devonte said. He thought of all of the things he could improve with the blade. The amethyst relic, his waterproof camera, and Allen's Mini Cooper came to mind.

"No wonder the forest and seaplane were shining like that," Allen remarked. It was all starting to make sense now. The Crocea Mors was not desolating the objects and things around them. Instead, it was improving upon them and making them better.

"Unfortunately, it has recoil and has to recharge every eight hours," Monique sighed.

"Nevertheless, its ability is quite uncanny," She finished. They were now looking at the sword. It wasn't so useless after all.

CHAPTER 20

Unexpected Visitors

They continued analyzing the sword. It was no longer glowing like it was earlier. Instead, it seemed vacant of light or luminous energy.

"I used it completely yesterday," Monique said. "Made sure to improve the tracking device and all of the essential tools in my possession. I even improved the lab itself."

"That's nice to know," Devonte replied. "But how are we going to stop others from taking the sword from us?"

"Well, you see, in all my years of research, I have developed a special case that gives off a magnetic frequency. This frequency counteracts the frequencies of the relics," She responded.

"That way, those tracking devices won't be able to pinpoint their location once we have them...absolutely brilliant," Ivan said. He was now ready to go out and find the Silver Panflute.

Caesarion was probably rolling over in his grave at how long it was taking them to retrieve it.

"I've set a timer. It should be fully charged again in an hour and a half. At that time, we could probably order some lunch," Monique said.

"Who's up for wings?" Allen said.

"Cheers, that's a great idea," Ivan said.

"I'll have blue cheese with mine, please," Devonte said. Savannah was also nodding in approval. Allen selected an app on his phone and ordered some buffalo wings. He ordered a family pack, enough to feed them well. About 45 minutes passed, and then Monique caught sight of a vehicle with a green logo in the dash parked outside the door. Two buff men stepped out, holding two boxes inside of bags.

"Food's here," Monique alerted. Allen, Devonte, and Ivan glanced at the boxes, then back at her.

"This one's on me. My bad for the tracking device problem," she said. Monique pulled a twenty from out of her satchel. Devonte took a closer look at the two delivery men. It usually didn't take two people to deliver food. They were the same cable guys that had come to his house. It was Jim and Mike. He was now on alert. He was ready to pull out the amethyst at any sign of trouble. The two delivery guys walked up the steps, and Monique opened the door.

"Mind if we come in for a second?" said one delivery man. He was holding a small clipboard. '

"Alright," Monique responded. The two men barged in and handed her the clipboard.

"Please sign here," the other man said. He had the same grimacing face Devonte saw from at his house. Monique took the clipboard and paused for a second. She then signed the receipt and handed it back to the delivery man. After she signed the clipboard, they began to look around intently.

"Nice lab you've got here miss," the delivery man with the clipboard said, in a devious tone. "Who would've thought all of this would be here. From the outside, it looks just like an average apartment."

"It's a work in progress. I am simply a humble scientist trying to conduct research," Monique said sheepishly. Allen and Ivan were standing beside her.

"Then I suppose perhaps these are your assistants?" The other food delivery man inquired, looking at Ivan and Allen.

"Yes, they are," Monique muttered. "Not that that concerns you," She whispered.

"What was that...What did you say? It does concern us," he thundered. The two delivery guys took out two badges that Devonte couldn't recognize as counterfeit or real. "We are the D.D.O.Z., Defense Department of "Z" generation."

"I'm Mike, and he's Jim," Mike said.

"We're agents of an organization designed to protect," the other delivery man said. Mike grabbed the clipboard and looked at it carefully.

"She's signed it, sir," he said. After putting the bags of food on the counter, the two undercover agents began to look around.

"Hey! What are you doing? You can't just search my lab," Monique exclaimed. "You don't have a warrant!"

"Yes, we do actually," Jim said. "You've just signed it." He then proceeded to have a closer look around, moving beakers out of place and leaving no table unturned.

"That's not fair. She thought it was for the food we just ordered. This can't be legal," Allen huffed. The agent then made a grimacing face again.

"It was for both the food and warrant kid," the other agent said as he walked over towards the back. After moving around some of Monique's lab equipment, he found the Crocea Mors, encased in a special see-through case made of glass and a metal frame.

"Here it is. Oh yeah, we are back in business, baby," Jim boldly said as he grabbed the handle.

"Hey! That doesn't belong to you," Monique said as she almost busted into tears. She had worked very hard to find her first artifact. But now, it was being taken from her.

"Yes, it does," Mike said as he held up the clipboard. He then proceeded into the violet room.

"We have to do something," Allen said as he looked at Devonte. Devonte looked into his pocket. The amethyst was glowing brighter than ever. He then looked at Monique. She was in deep thought for a moment and then shook her head subtly as if telling him not to use the amethyst.

"Nothing in here, I guess that's all they've got," Mike grunted.

"We got what we came for. Let's get out of here. I'm thirsty, and I need a cold one," The other agent barked as they were about to head out. Monique grabbed a red Gatorade from a contraption that looked like a mini-fridge.

"If you're thirsty, I have a red Gatorade if you want," She offered.

"Ha-ha, thanks. Stay out of trouble, and maybe we won't mess up the place next time," Jim said as he snatched the Gatorade and hurried out the door.

CHAPTER 21

Shadow Seeker

"What did you do that for?" Allen asked skeptically. "You shouldn't be giving juice to random strangers. Especially strangers that take things from you."

"That wasn't just juice," Monique said in a hushed tone. "That was a serum I devised in my early years of experimenting. It has a potent juice taste; however, under all of the sugary goodness, it has a tracking capability."

"You put a tracking device in a drink?" Ivan said, astonished. "That's simply incredible. Those bloody thieves won't know what hit em."

"Now that's amazing," Savannah said.

"Quick-thinking, daughter of Nefertiti," Devonte acknowledged. Monique curtsied in her lab coat. She then walked over to a computer with a strange antenna attached to it. After logging in, she waited for a moment. Once everything was settled, she pin-pointed the location of her red beverage.

"But how did they know the relic was here in the first place?" Devonte asked. He was worried that they might find his relic.

"They must have tracked and saved its location from when I used it yesterday. Don't worry. I don't think their tracking device is nearly as advanced as mine. It probably can only track when huge energy surges are given off. Your relic works on a lesser scale," Monique assured.

"Alright, I hope so. Don't want them tracking me," Devonte said.

"They won't. You should be fine. Although the amethyst relic is powerful, it carries a smaller polarity than the other relics," Monique stated. "They won't be able to detect it unless its charge becomes stronger."

"Oh, alright," Devonte responded. "That's good. We don't need anyone else coming for us," Monique yawned and nodded in agreement.

"Now who's up to track down some relic thieves?" she said, now in a measured tone. She looked at the computer's monitor. The pin-pointed location was still moving.

"They must be still driving with the blade," Allen said.

"Once they stop, we'll be able to find the address of their headquarters," Monique said.

"Are you sure?" Devonte asked.

"Yeah, unless he uses the bathroom," Monique said. "Let's sit here and wait for a moment. In the meantime, we can locate the Silver Panflute."

"Great idea! That way we can kill two birds with one stone," Savannah said. After around 30 minutes, the pinpointed location stopped moving.

"Ah, we've got something," Ivan said. He was now giving his full attention to the computer monitor.

"What is it? Have they finally stopped?" Allen asked.

"Yes, indeed," Ivan responded. Allen looked at the computer monitor then looked at Monique. Her inventing and quick thinking had saved them once again from trouble.

"Then we don't have a moment to lose. Let's go!" Devonte exclaimed. He was ready to solve this mystery once and for all. They walked out of the lab and headed towards their cars. Monique pressed the button on her keys to unlock her lavender Lexus from afar. They looked at Allen's car.

"Let's take the Lexus," Monique said. They hopped in her lavender Lexus. It had seven seats. Monique and Savannah sat in the front. Ivan began texting his pet sitter, checking to see if his Terrier had gotten into any trouble. It turned out he notoriously did as usual. He had knocked over a couple of houseplants and had attempted an escape that failed.

"Blasted fluffy," Ivan whispered. He thought that his Terrier would behave while he was away. He was wrong. After reading this, he sent some apology texts and encouraged the pet sitter to enforce docile dominance.

"Maybe you should feed him more treats," Allen said, looking over Ivan's shoulder at the texts.

"I already tried that," Ivan sighed. "He always acts stubborn around strangers. It just gets worse when I'm not around." He then put his phone away in his pocket.

"He probably just wants to roam free in an open area," Savannah giggled.

"Huh? Don't think I've ever thought of that," Ivan said. "He was rather content this one time I took him to the old country house back in Europe. My father's goats very much enjoyed his company."

"Yeah, I guess he needs the open space every once in a while," Monique said. Ivan then took his phone back out. He texted his pet sitter one more time, asking her to take him out to a dog park. She agreed to his request, and he put his phone back away. They continued driving. Finally, they arrived at the location. They parked in a nearby free parking lot. The location turned out to be a warehouse at a city port. Devonte did not remember ever coming to a port in Illinois.

"According to my tracking device, they are inside of there," Monique said as she pointed to a large warehouse. It was a chilly autumn day, prime for shipping.

"I'll wait in the car just in case," Savannah said. Devonte peeped inside. The warehouse had a small side door near the entrance with a glass window. He saw machinery moving and people with hardhats working. He also spotted several forklifts moving crates. After scanning the room, he saw Jim and Mike, standing near a corner talking. Devonte could overhear what they were saying.

"Come on, Mike. We've got to ship this to the boss man soon. He doesn't like to wait," Jim said.

"Right," Mike agreed. He then lifted a wooden crate that was the same size as the contraption Monique had designed to hold the Crocea Mors.

"There it is," Devonte whispered. Monique, Allen, and Ivan were now crouched near the window.

"We should make our move before the crate gets locked up and shipped out somewhere, ultimately becoming hard to reach," Allen suggested.

"Good idea," Monique agreed. They creaked the door open and went inside.

CHAPTER 22

The Almond Eater

After going inside, they found an ample open space with workers moving about. They were wearing bright turquoise uniforms with green hardhats. Devonte, Allen, Ivan, and Monique hid behind a large crate. Devonte peeped his head out around it and looked discretely. He tied his twists back so that they wouldn't hang over and alert one of the workers. As he was looking, he saw the inner workings of the entire operation—the workers where putting supplies into boxes with inhumane speed. Then after packing them, they began transferring them into a separate room.

When the coast was clear, he motioned for them to move in closer behind another crate. Ivan looked around the crate this time. He saw an overseer in a glass room above. A man in a grey fedora was sitting in there, supervising all of the procedures. Iven scooched in for an even closer look. In his hand, the overseer had a pack of almonds. He was munching on them ferociously. Ivan then stopped peeping around the corner and retreated to the group.

"There's a man up there in the booth, watching the ins and outs of the whole place," he said.

"We'll have to be extra careful if we want to get that sword back," Devonte said. He then peeked around the corner, himself. He glanced over and saw Jim and Mike loading the crate with the Crocea Mors in it. They were loading it into the other room.

"I guess that is where the sword is being kept," Monique whispered. Inside the other room was a large metal machine with similar symbols as the amethyst relic on it.

"Oh no, I don't like where this is going," Devonte exclaimed. Monique then looked with him, inwards towards the other room. Allen and Ivan now peeped around the corner as well. The workers were bringing in boxes from that room's floor. They were lining them up and organizing them into sections.

"We need to get a closer look," Monique proposed. She knew that in order for this recovery operation to succeed, they would have to have a plan.

"How are we going to do that? This place is crawling with those bloody guards," Ivan acknowledged. He was certain that the sword's retrieval would take a lot more effort than they originally thought it would.

"Hey guys, over here," Allen whispered. They all looked back at Allen. He pointed at two uniforms lying in a workroom's closet. Workers and guards were moving about, blocking their way.

"Somehow we have to get in there without being seen," Devonte said.

"Don't worry I've played enough video games," Allen said. He looked into his wallet and took a quarter out of his pocket. He then rolled it along the floor.

"Hey! Who threw that? No foreign metal is allowed in this area!" a worker said. He ran towards the quarter as it rolled down the hall. Allen rushed into the workroom and snatched the uniforms swiftly before the worker picked up the quarter and turned around. He then brought them back to Devonte, Ivan, and Monique behind the large crate.

"I got them!" Allen whispered, happy that his video game knowledge had come in handy. He laid the uniforms down. They were both green men's sized uniforms. On the uniform, the Oze logo was imprinted in big, bold letters.

"I don't think I can fit that," Monique said.

"Me neither mate," Ivan said. Allen and Devonte looked at each other and knew that it was up to them.

"You know what we have to do," Allen said. "You guys can go back. We need to be in complete stealth mode for this mission. If we aren't back in the next hour, something went wrong."

"Monique, thank you for guiding us this far. I may have stumbled and messed up as I remembered who I was, but you helped me refresh my memories. I extend my gratitude to you for that," Devonte commended.

"Okay, okay, I get it, now go get that sword," Monique said.

"Make it in one peace mate. I want to show you photos of my da's goat farm when you get back," Ivan whispered happily. Ivan and Monique walked out of the warehouse quietly and sprinted back towards the lavender, Lexus.

"Alright, it's up to us," Devonte declared. They hid back behind the other large crate and swiftly slipped into the uniforms.

"Who would've thought?" Devonte said. "These guys just came by a few weeks ago to install a new cable box in our house."

"You too?? That's mad crazy," Allen said.

"Next time I'll watch out for them. We won't open the door unless we actually need a new cable box," Devonte sighed. He was very intrigued that his prediction had become true. The cable men were indeed there for other reasons.

"How could I have been so naïve? They walked into my home," Devonte muttered.

"It's not your fault, man. From what it looks like, these people are organized, it goes deeper than us. Let's Just focus and get the sword," Allen said encouragingly.

"You're right. Thanks, I needed that," Devonte responded. They were now fully dressed into the Oze uniforms. Devonte motioned for Allen to follow him quickly. They saw a line of workers packing items into boxes.

"Quick, let's fall in behind them," Allen said. They walked over to the workers and found two boxes. They could not believe what they found inside. There were hundreds of old electrical devices and equipment. Cell phones, TVs, radios, walkie talkies, even small tablets were packed in a rushed manner. It didn't look like they were purchased.

"Why are we moving there?" one grunt asked.

"Don't ask questions," an overseer growled. "The boss wants these found objects moved into the Evo-Room as soon as possible."

"Evo-Room? I wonder what that could be," Devonte thought. He found a box with some corded cell phones inside of it and grabbed it. Allen found a box with some tablets inside. The man who was eating the almonds came down from the overseer room and walked into the Evo-Room. They fell in line behind the others and followed.

CHAPTER 23

The Dozers Brotherhood

Allen and Devonte followed the line of workers and carried their boxes into the room. There were rows and rows of boxes and crates all organized in single file lines. They made their way to a close position on the left near other workers. The man with the almonds saw a nearby trashcan and discarded his snack. He then proceeded towards a stage near the massive machine. After making his way up, all of the workers saluted him.

"Best not to attract attention," Allen whispered. Allen and Devonte, wearing their disguises, saluted as well. After a brief moment of silence, the boss walked up to a podium. He unruffled a few note cards and stood proud and tall. All of the workers with boxes leaned in close in expectancy and anticipation. Devonte looked near the stage and saw the man with the thick mustache and grey collar shirt from the Summer Solstice festival. He also saw the man with the orange top hat who wielded the megaphone. They were standing behind him. After clearing his throat, the man at the podium began.

"Welcome, gentlemen! Welcome, my comrades! Welcome all members of the esteemed Dozer's brotherhood!" he boomed. Everyone stood up and began clapping and cheering.

"Let it be known...That Today...History is being made," he said. "We were almost thwarted in our grand scheme." He pressed a button on his clicker and started showing a slideshow. A picture of Allen, Devonte, Ivan, Monique, and Savannah appeared. The crowd began to boo and hiss aggressively.

"But, no matter, the problem has been solved. They won't be bothering us anymore," he said with a diabolical grimace, as he changed the slide. The next slide showed pictures of the installed cable boxes in Allen and Devonte's homes. It also showed the food boxes in Monique's lab. The crowd hooted and hollered in a rowdy fashion.

"They thought they could think freely and create on their own, foolish children. Let us distract them. Let us dilute their minds with their enticing sweet quick fix. Their very own beloved media," he continued. Some of the crowd began raising cell phones and TV's and cheering in unison.

"As you can see, this month, we have made excellent progress towards our task...towards our affliction..." he went on. "We have acquired hundreds of items far and wide to aid in our campaign." A worker was chuckling next to Allen.

"Without paying for them," the worker laughed.

"Today marks the day that we execute! Today marks the day that we take action!" he began escalating his voice and then paused. The speaker then looked down and stood in deep thought for a moment. Allen and Devonte peered at each other for a moment, hoping that they weren't spotted.

"This is our mission, all that we've built...all that we are...We will suppress creativity and originality, unlike our own! We will take and enforce only what we are comfortable with onto the world!" he said.

He then pulled a lever. The box with the Crocea Mors began to open mechanically. As it opened, a reflective glow was shining from it again. This time it was amplified, and the light was brighter than before. Suddenly something was happening to the items in the boxes. Devonte and Allen began to see the items in the boxes shimmering in the same fashion the leaves did on Christmas island.

"Oh no," Allen whispered in horror.

"Our logistics company has access to hundreds across the globe. We will distribute and dispense our amazing arts and culture onto this poor lost, misguided world," the speaker said.

"They're using the blade to upgrade stolen equipment," Devonte said. As soon as he said this, the items in the boxes were now slightly levitating and began to change. Cell phones began to have fewer buttons. The tablets were becoming thinner. TV's began to curve and blink on with higher resolutions.

"We will then sell all of these products for profit. All proceeds will go towards our mission, and the sequence will repeat!" The speaker then added. His microphone also began to change. Allen and Devonte backed away from the boxes. They slowly weaved out of the large crowd and turned towards the door. Two workers were standing there, blocking the exit. They walked back towards the boxes.

"I...Omar... leader of our great organization will enforce regularity!" "With this beloved relic on our side...we will be unstoppable!" Omar yelled fervently. His microphone, now upgraded, was amplifying his voice even more. The crowd was now on their feet, caught in an uproar of applause and shouting. Devonte and Allen began shouting and clapping as well, so as not to be perceived as outsiders. After Omar finished delivering his monologue, the lever jerked out of place. Electronic devices in the audience began to stop floating. The Crocea Mors then ceased to give off its radiant glow. The mysterious magic and process of the Evo-Room came to a halt.

"Willy! What happened?" Omar yelled at the man with the orange top hat.

"Sir, we must give the blade some time to recharge," the man with the orange top hat said defeatedly.

"Then have it done, find a way to speed up the process!" he aggressively exclaimed. He then looked at the man with the thick mustache.

"You! James! Start working on finding that panflute! We don't want any hindrances in our operation," Omar boomed. He then said the words "Semper ad meliora." The sword mechanically moved below, into a locked, hidden chamber.

"Will do, sir," James said. He then straightened his collar and walked offstage out of a side door.

"My comrades...my close companions...We must bring regularity to the world! We must organize, label, and package these items, now...of increased value," he decreed. The workers now turned their attention to their boxes. The devices inside, once of little to no retail value, had turned into refined, sophisticated apparatuses.

"We will return here, at 15:00 to complete our assignment...our great burden. Next time around, be sure to bring goods that are even bigger and better!" Omar laughed maliciously. "Meeting dismissed." The workers that were blocking the exit moved aside. The crowd moved their boxes back out of the Evo-Room. They walked towards a large storage room with freshly painted, bright metal shelves. Allen and Devonte followed them deeper into the warehouse.

CHAPTER 24

Nocturnal World

They made their way into the storage room. They saw workers packing boxes into larger boxes. A team of workers was labeling boxes and organizing them by weight and number of items contained. Machines and cranes were then moving them into their designated numbered sections, respectively. Eight computer technicians were then typing in expected shipping dates into eight tablets. They were followed by four interns specially trained to confirm the shipping dates.

Devonte and Allen followed behind the workers and proceeded to put their boxes into the pile. They then walked swiftly towards through the crowd towards the exit before anyone could notice. Suddenly one worker looked at Allen.

"Oh. Where do you think you're going, mister??" he said. Allen looked back, petrified with fear.

"Uh well, I..." Allen stammered.

"You dropped your nametag," The worker said. He then gave Allen his nametag and smiled happily.

"Um, Thanks," Allen said.

"Happy to help," the worker smiled, moving along. He then paused for a brief moment. He looked back at Allen and Devonte walking, then shook his head and continued walking. After seeing how organized the operation was, Allen and Devonte began to worry. The Crocea Mors was safely protected in a locked, voice-activated, hidden safe. They definitely would not be able to retrieve the blade at this rate.

"There's no way we can reach that," Allen sighed. "We don't have the tools or equipment to combat such an organized arsenal."

"Not yet, at least..." Devonte said in a hushed tone. They made their way out of the storage room and crept slowly towards the exit. Devonte and Allen crept past the overseer room, where Omar was eating the almonds. They crept past the crates that they were once hiding behind and made their way out of the door whence they came. They slipped out of the uniforms.

"We have to warn the others before it's too late. We have to get to the Silver Panflute," Devonte said. He checked his watch. The time was already 4:30 p.m. Monique, Ivan and Savannah weren't there. They began to tread swiftly down the sidewalk. Allen then pulled his cell phone out of his pocket and called Monique. After four long rings, she picked up the phone as if she were busy doing something important.

"Where are you guys? We have to get out of here!" Allen shouted. Cars were driving by as they walked along.

"Well, you see, Ivan's pet sitter said his Terrier was causing trouble, so we went over there to handle that. Then we went to grab some food, and they messed up Savannah's order...that place is on our list now," Monique went on.

"What, Ivan's Terrier caused trouble? A messed-up order?" Allen asked irately. "We have more pressing problems than that now. Tell her Devonte." He then handed the phone to Devonte.

"They are an organization called the Dozers. An establishment... a brotherhood designed to...suppress creativity...and..." Devonte paused in anguish and disbelief.

"Go on. What else?" Monique asked. "Your voice sounds unsure. You sound defeated. What is it?"

"It's the sword," Devonte said softly. "We won't be able to obtain it on our own. We're going to need some serious firepower to get it out of there."

"What do you mean by that," Monique said, sounding perplexed.

"We're going to need the Silver Panflute..." Devonte said. He was now talking in a hushed tone. "Whatever it does...whatever secrets it beholds...we need to get it now before it's too late..."

"I'll be over there right away. We had to go and withdrawal a twenty out of the bank for the sitter. She only works with cash," Monique explained.

"Hurry, we have to get out of here before someone spots us," Devonte said declaratively. He then said goodbye and gave Allen back his cellphone.

"Looks like they won't be back as soon as we thought," he sighed. "We have to lay low until they get back to this side of town. Allen let out a sigh of disappointment.

"We just got out of there, and now we're still stuck," Allen complained.

"Sometimes, it's like that. We'll be alright," Devonte said, reassuring Allen.

"Whatever, if you say so," Allen responded. As they walked on the sidewalk, they began to see a group of stores lined down the block. There was a shoe store, a mattress store, and a super-center for electronics and appliances. All had the suffix "Oze" in them. The smaller stores were cleverly named Shooze, and Cozy Snooze. The supercenter for electronics had a large sign that read: "Oze: Business Class Cable and Ethernet." There was also an "Oze" cell phone repair shop nearby.

"I can't believe we didn't recognize this before," Devonte exclaimed. "This whole time, we were fooled."

"It's absolutely insane how deep this goes," Allen said in agreement. They looked on in horror as people were venturing into the stores buying shoes, upgraded phones, TVs, and clothes that they didn't need.

"We have to tell others about all of this. This is mad wild," Allen exclaimed. Devonte nodded his head in agreement. Just then, a brief flashback flashed across his mind. Again, this one felt different from the others. He was on a beach next to a port. Macedonian centurions with horses were traveling towards a large vessel. They were then loading cargo onto the large vessel.

The crew was hauling freight and moving spice crates containing ginger, cinnamon, and pepper.

"We must get these back to base. Caesar will be pleased." a Macedonian commander said. He then looked over towards the deck of the ship staring intently in Devonte's direction. He then snapped out of his flashback.

Allen didn't even bother to ask if he was alright. By now, it had become a regular occurrence. They then continued down the sidewalk. Devonte then felt a pulse inside of his left pocket. He looked down to see the amethyst. It was radiating its bright violet hue again. He looked back to see two workers from the warehouse following them.

"We've got company," Devonte said.

CHAPTER 25

The Chase

Allen looked back. The two people following them were quite a distance away, but Devonte could tell that they were Dozers because of their bright turquoise uniforms. The green hardhats also gave it away.

"They wouldn't run in broad daylight. That would definitely cause suspicion," Devonte said.

"We have to get out of here before they catch up to us," Allen remarked. He was now clutching his phone for dear life. He texted the group chats encouragingly, asking Monique to please hurry over. The three text bubbles floated, indicating she was typing. They then disappeared. Devonte looked back again. The two Dozers began to transition into a speed walk.

"I stand corrected. They've begun to pick up the pace," Devonte said concerned. "How far are they?"

"I don't know. Monique was typing something, but then she stopped," Allen muttered. They were now caught on a whim. A decision had to be made. Fight or Flight? Just then, two more Dozers came from around a corner, joining the pursuit of Allen and Devonte. Their pace quickened. Allen and Devonte quickened their pace as well. They were beginning to catch up.

"What are we going to do? We're outnumbered," Allen said frantically.

"Quick! In there!" Devonte said. They weaved through other pedestrians and walked into a side alley. It was a dead end. The Dozers followed them inside.

"Thought you could get away, huh?" One worker said. Allen and Devonte were backed into a corner.

"I don't know what you're talking about," Allen said.

"Don't play dumb. We know who you are," one Dozer said.

"Our shipments are never disorganized," another Dozer said. "We noticed two boxes that were left in the wrong place and watched camera footage of you two sneaking around."

"Uh oh," Devonte thought.

"Using face recognition technology, we just acquired through an upgrade, we were able to match your face in our advertising databases," the Dozer snarled.

"I knew I shouldn't have ordered those headphones online," Allen said. He only wanted better sound quality, not his face in a database.

"Turns out, y'all are the same two rascals from the slideshow," he laughed mischievously. They then moved in closer. Two Dozers took out music boxes similar to the one they encountered at Christmas Island. They began to play the melody of a cradlesong.

"Hurry, use the relic!" Allen exclaimed. Devonte pulled out the relic. It was shrouded in a mysterious ultraviolet light that was brighter than the last time. The Dozers were still walking closer.

"Stay back," Devonte said.

"How does the boy have a relic? Take it and make him pay!" another Dozer grunted. They continued playing the solemn, somber cradlesong. They walked even closer. Bricks began to dislodge themselves from the alley walls.

"Hand it over, kid, and you'll only get hurt a little bit." a Dozer laughed. After he said this, a brick then launched at Allen and Devonte's feet. It smashed, making a loud sound.

"That was a warning shot, the next one won't be as far from its target," one Dozer chuckled.

"Now we'll ask politely again. Hand over the relic!" he repeated. They were now about to close in.

Before the Dozers could surround them, a tremendous burst of energy exploded from him and the relic. It became an intense shockwave of ultraviolet light and blasted the Dozers back towards the edge of the alley. Devonte was yelling in agony as this energy was released. A radiant circle appeared above his head, and he was motionlessly levitating above the ground for a short while. Allen stood behind him with gawking eyes. The attackers were now knocked out, and their uniforms had lost their integrity. Allen looked closely at their torsos. They were still breathing. A few moments passed, and they came to. They saw Devonte hovering with the small sun above his head.

"I've...never seen anything like that," one Dozer whimpered. He sat on the ground, petrified with fear. This occurrence was way out of their paygrade. They were not used to having the people they intimidated, answering back in such a magnitude of ability.

"We...have to tell Omar," another stammered.

"Let's get out of here," one Dozer cried. They fled the alley and rushed back towards the Dozer warehouse. The Amethyst relic stopped glowing.
The small sun disappeared from above Devonte's head, and he landed firmly on the ground.

"How did you do that?" Allen asked curiously. He now had many questions.

"The amethyst's powers must be getting stronger as more of my memories come back to me," Devonte said in a hushed tone. He was now looking intently at the amethyst relic. Hieroglyphics were appearing on it. He briefly saw an eagle-shaped crest that quickly disappeared.

"That's mad crazy. I didn't think all that Egyptian nonsense Monique was talking about, would help us out," Allen said.

"I wonder what this means," Devonte said, as he paused for a moment. "Am I...really a descendant of Akhenaten?" With this being said, Allen had an important realization.

"That would mean that all of the other relics would best belong in the hands of their descendants as well," he said in a hushed tone. Allen was now stirred with interest. He wanted a smaller relic of his own.

"Well, your highness," Allen joked. "We should get back to Ivan, Monique, and Savannah and bring them up to speed."

"Alright," Devonte said. They walked out of the alley and back onto the sidewalk. Allen took out his phone and began dialing Monique's number once more. She instantly picked up.

"We're around the corner," she said calmly.

"And not a moment too soon," Allen replied. They then walked out of the alley and towards Monique's lavender Lexus.

CHAPTER 26

Truth Revealed

They sprang into the lavender Lexus with more newfound bravery in their hearts and determination in their eyes. Monique pulled off and started driving towards her lab.

"You're not going to believe what happened," Allen exclaimed.

"What, happened?" Ivan said munching on a cool wrap. Monique and Savannah also had food.

"After we explained what happened at the warehouse, we were attacked by some of the dozers."

"Well, it wasn't really much of an explanation. My fault, I was caught in the moment," Devonte acknowledged.

"It's okay. We just need to get all of the facts presented here and now," Monique said. "Bring us all up to speed."

"Alright," Devonte nodded and agreed. "Well you see, the Dozers are using the Crocea Mors to upgrade stolen possessions into unnecessary items."

"That's horrible," Monique said with a gasp.

"It gets worse from there. They are then reselling the stolen goods to naïve people. They are left ultimately hypnotized into a cycle of purchasing unnecessary products," Devonte continued.

"What a poor use of the blade. Their malicious endeavors are not good," Monique said with a hint of ferocity.

"They are also using media to distract people and suppress originality that is unlike their own," Allen added.

"That's so not cool," Savannah said. Monique continued driving. Devonte then looked at Allen.

"Also, it turns out Devonte really is a descendant of that pharaoh you were talking about earlier," Allen mentioned.

"What happened? Was it the Amulet? Was it amplified?" Monique asked as she bombarded them with questions.

"Yes...Wait. How did you know?" Devonte inquired.

"I've been studying these relics for a long time. I know most of their secrets and wonders if their phenomena were ever recorded on papyrus paper," Monique declared proudly. Devonte looked at her in the mirror of the Lexus. She was looking back.

"You must be regaining your memories! I knew you would," Monique said happily. "Your body must have reverted back to its true protective state as soon as he came in contact with the relic."

"He also started floating," Allen added.

"Fascinating! Do tell me more, did he have a spherical shaped object above him? Devonte, were you glowing?"

"Yeah, a little bit. It was like I could feel a sudden burst of energy. It was invigorating yet terrifying at the same time," Devonte said.

"Simply amazing," Monique said and began driving in a jubilant way.

"Also, we have to get rid of anything that they delivered to our doors within the last couple of days. Apparently, they are using those to do detective work on us," Allen reminded.

"How are we going to get back there in time? They are planning to use the blade again soon," Allen reminded.

"Then that leaves us no choice. We have to get to the Silver Panflute," Devonte said.

"Well, the good news is, we've discovered where its located," Ivan said fervently. It's located on Charles Mound right here in Illinois.

"We have to climb a mountain??" Allen said.

"Of course. You thought the ancestors would just give the relics to us that easily?" Monique laughed. "It's more of a very large hill really. We are lucky it is in such a close location."

"A historian must have needed money and sold it on accident. Some hippie must have then acquired it and left it on one of their hiking escapades," Devonte supposed.

"That's tough," Allen said. He was still shocked at the fact that they had to climb a mountain.

"We will be fine," Monique said. "It will be a trip worth-while."

"Alright," Allen sighed.

"We must hurry. We have to get to it before a lackey from the Dozers does," Monique said now in a more serious tone. She sped up and they drove on.

They reached the base of the mountain. Monique parked her lavender Lexus at a designated parking area. Everyone hopped out. A sparrow flew overhead. It gave off a call of melancholy. Devonte checked his wrist. The time on his watch was now 6:30 p.m. There was a trail leading up the large hill. Monique took out her now upgraded tracking device.

"I guess we have to follow that trail. It probably leads to the place where the Silver Panflute was lost," Monique said.

"Okay, let me put on some bug spray first," Savannah said. "This reminds me of the time I went camping with my cousin."

Allen, Devonte, Ivan, Monique, and Savannah strode up the trail. Along the way, they passed by good spots for campgrounds, and decent places to hunt small game. They then went by an overpass. Wildlife was traveling over it. After some time hiking up the hill, they then came across an abandoned cabin. They ignored it and kept walking, following the directions given by Monique's tracking device.

Eventually, they stumbled upon the peak of the Charles Mound. In the center of the mound, was a wooden box with a note attached to it.

"That must be it! Let's grab it and get out of here," Allen said.

"Wait, we're going to need to check the note out first before we take it," Monique said. She then carefully picked up the note and read it.

"*Dear traveler may this help you in your journey. It helped me in mine,*" from, Stanley.

"Yep he was a hippie," Devonte said.

He then opened the wooden box. He couldn't believe what was inside. To his surprise, it was the legendary Silver Panflute.

CHAPTER 27

The Silver Panflute

Allen, Ivan, Devonte, Monique, and Savannah stood in awe as the Silver Panflute reflected light as if it were made of glass. It had streams of ultraviolet light pouring out of its silver pipes.

"It is incredible," Ivan said in fascination. He then reached down to take hold of it. As soon as his fingertips touched it, it gave off a radiant golden flash. They looked down at the Silver Panflute. There was a mixture of hieroglyphics and Latin phrases engraved on it. One large Latin phrase read, "Condemnant quo non intellegunt."

"What does that mean?" Savannah asked.
Devonte pulled out his phone and put a Latin to English translator in the search bar.

"It says, they condemn that which they do not understand," Devonte said. He then put his phone away.
Suddenly Monique became quiet, deep in thought.

"Of course! Why haven't I thought of that?" Monique exclaimed. She was now pacing in a circle.

"What? What is it?" Allen said.

"I know what the panflute does now," Monique said. They began walking back towards the lavender Lexus.

"In all my years studying the artifacts, I can't believe I overlooked this concept," she said. Monique was now looking at Ivan attentively.

"Caesarion was of mixed ethnicity, part Macedonian and part Egyptian," she continued.

"Condemnant quo non intellegunt," Monique repeated. "They condemn that which they do not understand...The Silver Panflute has the power to help people understand."

"Cleopatra gave the Silver Panflute as a gift to her son Caesarion so that he could be understood by both cultures; so that people of both tongues could understand him," Ivan now held the Silver Panflute close to his chest.

"This is special. I'll guard it with my life," Ivan said zealously. They continued walking down the Charles Mound, walking past the wildlife they had seen earlier. They passed the abandoned cabin. Allen, Ivan, Devonte, Monique, and Savannah walked down the mound pondering how far they had come. A boy who had lost his memories now had become a conscious warrior. A girl who was once misunderstood gained increased perception and understanding. The man of blended heritage, once longing for acceptance, now had solid, reliable friends. A girl who lacked adventure had now found it. And the sneakerhead who once feared change was now a driving force of it.

As they were descending, Ivan began to see a figure in the distance. The figure had a thick mustache and was wearing a grey collar shirt with matching grey gloves. It was James, the commander under Omar in the Dozers. Omar had sent him to carry out a relatively simple task. He had come back to stop the Encraty once and for all. James stared at them for a moment. He was holding the Crocea Mors. The landscape was dead silent. Devonte pulled out the Amethyst relic and stepped forward. His body began to change again.

This time, hieroglyphics appeared on his arms. He returned to his previous form and was emitting pulses of ultraviolet light from his body and the relic again. Ivan walked forward as well, standing beside him. Savannah, Allen, and Monique stood in the back.

James stepped forward. He held the blade in a reverse sword grip. A breeze, from winds above the mound, blew by a maple leaf. There were no words spoken; there were only the inaudible expressions given off through faint looks and gestures. Monique looked intently at Devonte. He looked back and nodded as if to promise they would be victorious. The faint flicker of tranquil salmon-colored paint had seeped into the canvas above the horizon. Destiny had led them to this moment.

Everything they had experienced, every trial they had overcome, had to be experienced in order for them to reach this point. There was an ambiance of intensity in the atmosphere.

All of the times they were misguided, all of the times that they came up short, none of that mattered now. It was now or never. They would be forced to leap into the unknown. They would be forced to take action and uncover the intricate mysteries shrouding the legendary ancient Silver Panflute.

Ivan took the Silver Panflute back out of the box. He held it firmly in his hand. There was a rumble of storm clouds overhead, forming in the sky. Savannah and Monique were looking onward in wonder and astonishment. Gold Egyptian wristwear appeared on Ivan's wrists. A gold chain coated in hieroglyphics appeared around his neck. A roman tunic emerged around his waist. He was the spitting image of Caesarion.

Ivan and Devonte advanced forward. Nearby patches of grass began to catch fire from the heat radiating from the sphere above Devonte's head. They were walking in a steady, powerful manner as if they were caught in slow motion. It was the walk of two successors who had reclaimed their authority. It was the walk of two kings, who had reclaimed their throne. As they were moving closer, Devonte began to levitate, similar to when he and Allen were cornered in the back alley after being caught off-guard in the Dozers encounter.

However, James held his ground. A faint glow of the Crocea Mors glistened in his presence. The shimmering light surrounded it once again, and the sound of metal particles shifting reverberated connected by the handle to his hand. He did not seem phased at all by the light show given off by Allen and Devonte. Omar had given him a mission. It was in his best intentions to complete it or die trying.

Ivan and Devonte inched even closer. Their tremendous energy was getting stronger. Ivan's tunic was now starting to become Macedonian Centurion armor. A shining breastplate materialized onto his chest. Macedonian leg guards began to form protecting the front side of his Achilles tendon. James was now bracing himself. Was this...fear in his eyes? He had begun to clench the sword with all of his might.

They now began to see James in a different light. He was not the vast, terrible, evil adversary that they had anticipated him to be. He was just a person doing what he was told to do. He did not know any better.

A hush fell over the land. Suddenly, Ivan began to play the Silver Panflute.

CHAPTER 28

Solemn Song

As Ivan began to play, Allen's previous doubts began to disappear suddenly. The once prevalent fears had changed into optimism.

"Look at that! The panflute is shining so bright!" Allen said. An overlay of gleaming luminosity surrounded the panflute as he played. Each pipe held a harmony and gave off a tone of sorrow but benevolence across the realm. He was right. The panflute was bright. While Ivan played, a mysterious aurora filled the air, causing James to take two steps back. He was now swaying from side to side. He looked dizzy as if he were going to collapse. His once strong stance had deteriorated into a faltering stumble. James' tough demeanor was beginning to come apart at the seams.

He drifted into a brief paralysis of shock from the Somber Song. Allen and Devonte looked at him for a moment. They then proceeded to power down from their abstract forms. Devonte's spherical object vanished, and he stopped levitating. Ivan's Macedonian tunic and Egyptian wristwear had returned to his regular clothes. They were then left standing in front of James. Stunned from the sound of the Silver Panflute, he then dropped the sword. He slowly turned around and walked away. Allen picked up the sword and held it in his hand for a second. Monique, Allen, Ivan, Savannah, and Devonte watched as James made his way back towards the parking lot.

They followed him from a distance as he mounted a retro motorcycle with black leather seats. He fired the ignition on his bike and sped off into the distance as if he were shaken and confused...They did not bother following him. Allen then handed the sword back to Monique.

"Well, we got the sword back..." he said. "I wonder what happened to that guy. Where was he off too in such a hurry?'

"I believe our foe has had a sudden change of heart," Monique said with a smile.

"What makes you say that?" Devonte asked.

"It was the panflute," Ivan said in a hushed tone. "When I played it, I could see the reaction change in his eyes."

"What do you mean?" Allen said with a hint of curiosity in his tone.

"I could visibly see the change in his face. His expression went from an unmovable resolve, to fear, and then to an alternate perspective," Ivan said. Monique looked at them for a second.

"So, my prediction has become correct?" Monique inquired.

"Yes, apparently the flute does have the ability to provide manners of understanding," Ivan said.

"So, what are you saying?" Savannah asked.

"If my prediction is correct... James has changed from being bad to becoming a potential ally," Monique said.

"Wherever he his...wherever he might be... I hope that we meet again," Devonte said in an earnest tone. They hopped into the lavender Lexus. Allen and Ivan placed the newfound relics into the back of her trunk. The digital clock of Monique's car indicated that it was now 8:38 p.m. There was the cry of a bat screeching overhead, entering the new night.

As they drove back to Monique's lab, it was rather quiet. They were exhausted. Their expended energy had to recharge. Ivan was now arranging for a car to pick him up from Monique's lab and drop him back at his apartment.

"We should rest for the night and then prepare our next move. Everyone, rest up," Monique said.

"You don't have to tell me twice," Allen said. He was now leaning in his seat curled up, about to take a "phat" nap. He had already texted his mother, alerting her that he would be home soon. Savannah was on her phone, scrolling through text messages. Her cousin would be coming back late. She told Savannah that a spare key was hidden under the doormat.
Ivan was knocked out. He fell fast asleep after expending so much energy from using the panflute. Devonte watched carefully out of the window. The night was not over just yet. He sat

erect and vigilant, as they drove by buildings, movie theaters, and businesses that were unmistakably owned by the Dozers. They still had work to do.

Finally, they arrived at Monique's lab. Ivan, waking up before him, nudged Allen.

"Get up, mate. We're here," he said. Allen jolted awake.

"Huh, woah, I thought you were asleep," Allen said in disbelief.

"We're here," Ivan repeated. He was now looking around the parking lot looking for the ride he had called. "My ride is running rather late."

"That's tough," Allen said and patted Ivan's shoulder. Savannah got out of the car. Her red hair was slightly matted from falling asleep against the window seat. Monique stepped out of the car. Her dreadlocks were drifting somewhat with the wind of the night. After looking around for a moment warily, she unlocked the back of her trunk. Inside were the two essential relics that they had obtained. Allen carried the Crocea Mors sword over his shoulder, and Ivan held the wooden box with the Silver Panflute.

Monique unlocked the entrance of her lab, and they walked inside. Ivan and Allen brought the relics inside. Devonte followed closely behind. After they made their way inside, they went to the room next to the violet room. Monique opened the room with a keypad. The door then opened swiftly. She brought the relics inside the room.

She placed the Silver Panflute in a similar containment unit as the one she had designed for the Crocea Mors. She connected a large cable to its glass case and plugged it into a moni-tor that could read the energy levels it was giving off. This way, if its energy skyrocketed or peaked abnormally, she could in-crease the counter charge of the case and cancel out its signal. She then put the Crocea Mors in a spare glass case that she had designed for it as a contingency plan. Monique knew that someone might try to take it from them, so she had made an extra in preparation for such an incident occurring.

She then locked the room back with a keypad. Monique then led Ivan and Allen towards a mini-fridge compartment that she had created in her lab's previous upgrade. There was more Gatorade mixed with sprite concealed inside. They both began drinking the beverages from the hidden compartment she had shown them. After they had their fill, they made their way towards the entrance. Ivan looked out of the lab window. His ride was now parked in front of the building.

"Welp, I'm off. Cheers. We'll meet again tomorrow, I sup-pose," Ivan said. He exited the lab and climbed into a grey sedan. He then rode off into the night. They came out of her lab. Monique locked the door back.

"Tomorrow," Monique repeated, her words echoing into the night. The moon was shining high above, a beacon of hope, in the twilight hour.

"Savannah, where did you say you were staying?" Monique said.

"My cousin's place," Savannah responded fervently. Monique handed her the phone, and she was now entering a long address. Allen and Devonte headed towards the mini cooper. They hopped in and buckled their seatbelts. Allen turned on his headlights and headed off towards their side of town. He played a bass boosted song at a low volume as they drove.

"I wish I could have kept that sword," Allen complained. "Unlike the Dozers, I actually buy the goods I need to upgrade," he said. Devonte then shook his head.

"You'll be alright, mane. That type of power shouldn't be used for just anything. We should save it for emergencies and for the lab," Devonte said.

"Yeah, I know. I guess you're right," Allen agreed. They then drove onto the expressway. A couple of muscle cars drove by, and it was evident they were out too late. As they drove, they passed by a few billboards. "Oze: Business Class Cable and Ethernet," one advertisement said.

"Of course. Their company really runs deep," Devonte said. Allen was also looking at the billboards as he drove.

"It is what it is, I guess. We have to change hearts and minds, one day at a time," Devonte said. They kept driving along the freeway. Allen and Devonte noticed two delivery trucks. One truck had the "Snooze" logo on it. The other was a mattress truck for "Cozy Snooze".

"All of this enterprise, wow, this system is a big deal," Allen said. "The Dozers have been busy."

"Can you turn that up?" Devonte asked as he pointed to the silver volume knob.

"Sure," Allen replied. He turned up the music on the radio. The bass boosted song had now changed into a different tune.

"You're listening to the Oze," The radio boomed. Devonte and Allen listened carefully to the lyrics. The song was promoting all of the ideals that the Dozers had instilled into society. New shoes, new phones, upgraded TVs, bigger and better stuff.

"Woah, I never noticed that before," Allen said. He then insistently turned the radio off.

"Yeah, we have some work to do," Devonte said. They got off the interstate and made their way back towards their side of town. Allen dropped Devonte off at his house.

"Do you want to meet at the lab early again?" Allen asked.

"How early are we talking?" Devonte laughed.

"We can meet at 2:00 p.m.," Allen responded.

"Bet," Devonte confirmed. He then unlocked his house with his bronze key.

CHAPTER 29

Memories Restored

The next morning Devonte woke up on the right side of the bed. He stretched his muscles and arose with delight. And to his relief, he no longer had a pain in his left temple. After feeling his forehead for a moment, he rushed to his bathroom mirror. The bruise was gone entirely. During his time spent in the Encraty, it had finally healed.

Devonte moved over towards his desk drawer. He dug through it recklessly and frantically. He remembered the pictures of baseball games, old basketball trophies, and even pins from academic achievements.

Devonte looked out of his window. The world was starting to make sense again. He remembered how he had met Monique at an archeology internship that he managed to acquire. He remembered how he had accidentally bumped into her in the hall and knocked over her books, in a rush. He helped her out. They became the closest of research partners and, more importantly, the closest of friends.

They were working diligently in Monique's lab, combining ancient knowledge of the artifacts, with modern-day innovations. They were developing technology that could forever change humanity. Devonte remembered that they had figured out a way to separate elements and rearrange them into eco-friendly machines. Suddenly, his enthusiasm faded.

He also remembered what had happened that day at the park. A brief memory flashed across his mind.
He stood in a park next to Monique. She was holding a small suitcase with containers with blank labels inside of it.

"I need to get some samples of these maple trees for our research," Monique said calmly.

"Alright," Devonte said. They passed a metal park bench and made their way into a temperate forest of park trees. As Monique began collecting samples with her scalpel, a cool breeze blew by. Suddenly, it began to sprinkle. Cool water droplets began pattering off of the leaves.

"We should make it quick, it is starting to drizzle," Devonte said. The drizzle now picked up into a light rain.

"Almost finished," Monique said. The light rain now suddenly picked up into a harsher rain. High winds blew, carrying updrafts of airstreams. The occasional roar of faraway thunder began to rumble in the distance.

"Your lab coat is getting soaked. I left my umbrella back at the lab," Devonte said, now bothered by the sudden change from temperate weather.

"Stop whining. I have a poncho in my car if you want to go get it," Monique said, continuing her work. The rains picked up their tempo, as an orchestra does when conducted by a composer. The thunder continued to rumble, even louder than before.

"I'm serious we should go home this weather isn't good," Devonte said, now yelling over the fierce call of the wind. Monique could no longer hear him. The Trees, he once thought to be firm and immovable, began to shake violently, as if they were blades of grass. The once gentle breeze had become a hurricane of violent turbulence. The sky was relentlessly roaring with agitation.

It became a crescendo in the symphony of nature. Devonte ran towards Monique's car. He was now determined to get that rain poncho. Monique still determined to collect the maple tree samples, did not follow him. He jogged towards a different section of the park, looking for the place where Monique was parked. As he walked, the weather increased its ferocity.

"It is unusual to have weather that was this intense here...I wonder what could have caused this, all of a sudden?" he thought. He continued walking in the direction that he thought the parking lot was. Several trees had shifted their positions, and now he was beginning to get worried. The rain was pouring now. His clothes were no longer dry.

He moved past a roundabout where bikers usually traveled. Today, there were no bikers in sight. Devonte saw an abandoned birdhouse. It once had a family of red cardinals occupying it. There was no sign of anything living there now. A young couple must have built it. Their initials were engraved into it, as well as the tree it resided on.

Devonte rushed on through the rain. He came upon a clearing in the dense forest. He walked out into the clearing, but it was the wrong parking lot. He must have gotten lost somewhere along the line in this heavy rain. He then proceeded to turn around and head back. Maybe he could meet back up with Monique and convince her to look for Maple samples on another day. After coming up with this thought, he headed back, with a new directive.

Just then, a small-scale branch fell from above and hit Devonte on his left temple. He fell to the ground under a tree and began to blackout. As he was blacking out, he noticed that a well-dressed figure in the distance, holding a blue amulet. He then vanished. Monique ran towards Devonte, and everything faded. He then snapped out of his flashback.

"Woah, so that's how it happened," Devonte said. "Someone out there already has the Amulet of Hatshepsut. And they used it against us that day." He now clutched the amethyst relic with great care. It was now his first form of defense against those trying to stop their research and recovery. Devonte took the note that came with the relic, out of his drawer. Surprisingly, he still didn't know who this "B" person was. The person who had sent him the relic had to be someone he could trust. They had to be aware of everything going on. He then walked out of his room and down his stairs. His little brother Ethan was waiting for him. He ran straight towards Devonte with a very big smile. He then hugged Devonte.

"Devonte! I've missed you," Ethan said. Their mother was in the living room watching a cooking show on the old cable box. The other night, he had presented substantial evidence and convinced her to let go of the new cable box. It had almost all of the channels that the other cable box had. It was a product the Dozers used to promote their ideals of having more stuff. In reality, they would be fine with the items that they already had. Devonte would definitely meet with the others later to solve this problem once and for all.

"I've missed you too, little man," Devonte exclaimed, patting Ethan on the head. It had been a while since they had last seen each other. His vacation with the new comrades was running longer than he had expected. Devonte made his way to the living room and poured himself a bowl of cereal. They sat together talking about all of the great adventures he recently went on, zealously.

CHAPTER 30

The Fall of Omar

After catching up with his brother, Devonte checked the digital clock on the stove. The time was now 12:12 p.m.

"Well, I should be going. We have to go save the world," Devonte said. His mother looked at him and then laughed.

"Be safe out there. I don't want you coming home with any more concussions or amnesia," She remarked. Ethan looked up at Devonte with eyes of innocence and wonder.

"See you later, alligator," he said.

"In a while, crocodile," Devonte responded. "I'll be back soon," And then he headed out the door. Allen was already outside, waiting for him.

"Come on, we don't want Ivan to beat us there again," Allen exclaimed spiritedly.

"Right," Devonte nodded his head in agreement. They hopped in his mini cooper and sped off towards Monique's lab. He decided not to turn on the radio this time as they drove. It was a swift, silent ride downtown towards the lab. Allen cruised along in the fast lane, hoping he could make it there in time before Ivan had arrived. There was no real purpose for doing this, but he just liked to test how early he could arrive every once in a while.

They made it to Monique's lab. Once again, Ivan was already there.

"What? How!?" Allen exclaimed. Ivan looked at him and smiled.

"I schedule my rides on time," he said, holding up a watch on his wrist. He then observed as Monique pulled up with her lavender Lexus. Savannah was sitting in the passenger seat. They got out of her car and walked into the lab. Monique led them into the violet room. They sat down. Monique pulled out her tablet again.

"Alright, listen up," Monique started. "We have two of the major relics in our possession and one smaller scale relic. We have no excuse not to win. I expect to dismantle their operations today, once and for all."

"Let's do this!" Allen said.

Go team Encraty, Savannah exclaimed.

"Let's save the world," Devonte said in a hushed tone.

After giving her speech, Monique then went to the room with the relics. They were now fully charged and operational. She pressed a button on the side of the containment unit. The glass latched open. A mist of clear smoke escaped.

"I have to keep the relics at low temperatures so that the energy they conduct doesn't leak out," Monique said. Ivan then reached down and grabbed hold of the wooden box, containing the Silver Panflute. Allen then pulled the Crocea Mors out of its case. Ivan could feel the energy emitting from the panflute. The reflective pipes each played an important role in the pan flute's somber song of sorrow yet benevolence. After getting the relics ready, they walked out of Monique's lab towards her lavender Lexus. They took Monique's car again and drove towards the warehouse. They were prepared and ready to end this corrupted, systematic organization. The efficient cycle of prejudice would finally come to an end, here and now.

Devonte stepped out of the vehicle with the amethyst relic in his hand. Ivan held the panflute. Allen held the Crocea Mors blade in his hand. They walked towards the warehouse slowly.

"We'll wait back here," Monique said. "Wow, I wish I had the Necklace of Nefertiti," Savannah looked at her, confused. They waited in the lavender Lexus. A few moments later, she began explaining to Savannah the intricate history of the relics. As they came closer to the warehouse, they began to notice that it looked empty.

"That can't be right," Devonte said. "They were just working there the other day."

"Maybe they took the day off?" Allen asked.

"Not likely, it's not the weekend yet," Ivan added. They continued walking until they approached the side door entrance they had found earlier.

"We ought to be careful in here," Devonte said. "We don't know if they've set a trap for us or not."

"You're right. Let's be on the lookout," Allen agreed. They then opened the door to the warehouse. The door creaked open. It was quiet…Too quiet… The atmosphere was dark and gloomy. A single lamp was on overhead. All of the other lights were turned off, and they could not find the switch. An air of melancholy drifted.

"Keep your eyes, sharp mates," Ivan said encouragingly. They made their way into the shipping deck. Sections that once owned labelers, packaging crews, and computer technicians, were now barren. They saw a man sitting in a grey rolling chair. After walking closer, they realized that it was Omar himself.

"You're too late. I've already shipped the goods off into my other facility," Omar grinned.

"Where is that!" Allen asked.

"I'll never tell," Omar said now in a more serious tone. Ivan raised the Silver Panflute as if to say, "Watch it, bud."

"A mere bluff, I suppose. You don't even know how to use that thing," Omar said. This was all Ivan needed to hear. He took a step forward towards Omar. Ivan then pressed the Silver Panflute against his lips again and began to play its somber song. Suddenly, the lights in the warehouse started to flash on. The empty workbenches began to rattle. Ivan underwent his transformation again. This time another Latin phrase appeared upon the panflute. It read, "Veni, Vidi, Vici."

"I came, I saw, I conquered," Devonte thought as he recognized the phrase. As Omar heard the somber song of the Silver Panflute and saw these wonders and occurrences, his reaction shifted in the same manner that James did. He now stood stunned, speechless. It was as if he had now understood the magnitude of his wrongdoings.

"Please, forgive me," he said. Omar, now idle, handed Ivan and Devonte a folded slip of paper. "Take...this..." The folded slip of paper had coordinates on it. It had coordinates of the facility the devices were transferred to.

CHAPTER 31

Golden Eagle

Ivan and Devonte accepted the slip of paper and exited the warehouse. Omar was still lying there, paralyzed in shame and tremendous guilt. They left him there and did not intend to see that foul warehouse ever again. Omar would be left there forgotten and no longer seen by them.

They piled into Monique's Lexus

"What happened! Did you stop the Dozers?" Monique asked eagerly.

"Yes and no," Devonte said sadly. His response was not what they were expecting, and it had piqued their interests.

"What do you mean by that?" Savanah inquired.

"Well, you see, Omar, the president of the Dozers, was in there," Ivan explained.

"You stopped him, right?? Please tell me you stopped him," Monique said, now worried.

"The Silver Panflute has the ability to provide clarity and understanding," Devonte reminded. "Allen played it, and we believe Omar has had a revelation."

"He won't be helping the Dozers again anytime soon," Ivan declared.

"Don't be so naïve, be on the lookout for any signs of trouble you find," Monique said. After saying this, she pulled off back towards the lab.

As they drove by, Ivan pulled out his cell phone and began texting his pet sitter. His Terrier was finally starting to behave. It turns out, all he needed was a little space and some open air. The pet sitter sent back pictures of his Terrier behaving. The dog had learned to sit, rollover, and fetch.

Savannah was now frantically texting on her phone. Her cousin had started a travel club and was sponsoring young adventurers to get out and see the world around them. They would do so for a price of course.

Monique looked at the folded sheet of paper with the written warehouse coordinates. She then thought to herself for a moment. This would be an adventure for another time. They now began to cruise along towards Monique's lab. She was playing smooth jazz on the radio.

Sunshine began to pour in, and birds outside started chirping to the groove of the beat.

They made their way to her lab and put away the relics that they had recovered. They put the Silver Panflute back into its wooden box. They put the Crocea Mors back into the containment unit.

"Next time around, we should look for the Necklace of Nefertiti. We don't have to go after the other dozers right away," Monique said. "We should wait until we are fully ready."

"Agreed," Savannah concurred. "I wonder if I'll find a relic as well."

"From what I've seen so far, anything is possible," Devonte affirmed. They then exited the lab and went their separate ways home.

Allen dropped Devonte off at his house.

"That was wild man," Allen sighed. "But we finally stopped Omar."

"Yeah," Devonte said. "Who knew there was so much to uncover. It runs so much deeper than me losing my memories."

"That's for sure. We've got to be more careful from now on," Allen declared. Devonte and Allen then dapped and shook hands.

"Welp, it was fun, but I've got some orders to drop off," Allen said. "A new low bred's colorway just dropped." He took a shoebox out of his trunk and opened the box. A shiny pair of grey shoes were inside.

"Alright man, whatever you say," Devonte laughed. "I'll stick to my refurbished 12's." Allen took out a receipt from his pocket and put it inside of the shoe box.

"Alright, I'll catch you later," Allen said. He got in his Mini Cooper and sped off, listening to a new reggae song that he had discovered on his phone. The speakers in his Mini Cooper were now upgraded from the Crocea Mors that had sit in the back the other day. The upbeat tune blasted through the speakers that were now of greater quality.

"I wonder where he finds these songs," Devonte thought. They were always quite peculiar compared to the mainstream songs that everyone else streamed. "Maybe he has a special app."

Devonte walked back towards his house and decided to check their small mailbox. As he opened the mailbox, he saw that it was just junk. Inside the mailbox were some washing machine coupons, a campaign card for a politician no one heard of, and a few advertisement catalogs. He planned on discarding all of these items. Just then, Devonte heard the loud cry of a raptor overhead. He put the mail back into the mailbox and looked up. It was the golden eagle.

The golden eagle flew through the sky and perched itself onto a wooden telephone pole. It was staring intently at him. Devonte stared back with a gaze of wisdom and understanding. His insight and awareness had increased. The experiences and occurrences had shaped him and molded him into a fearless warrior.

The bird of prey then left its roost on the telephone pole. It hovered high over him for a moment and dropped a single brown feather from its esteemed plumage. It then flew off into the distance. Devonte picked up the feather. He then took out the amethyst relic. The hieroglyphic crest of the eagle appeared once again. It began to glow in a shimmering light...

Dear Reader,

"*Encraty: Mystery of the Silver Panflute*", is a merged work of both fact and fiction. It portrays various struggles of minorities and challenges many misconceptions through the usage of imagery and symbolism. The work was inspired by a letter than I received, from the Civil Rights leader John Lewis at age 15.

I am simply a young person trying to make the world a better place. Around me, I have seen many people who should expand their horizons and try to see the world from a new perspective. I serve as a slight guide on their path. A path of respecting cultural differences and differentiations of all peoples, without assumptions.

I hope this work was entertaining and informative. Although most of it is science fiction, there are various historical facts scattered throughout.

I plan on continuing this series when the time is right. If you enjoyed this book, please share it with close friends and family. This is made possible by your contributions.

I appreciate your support! Stay blessed.

Sincerely,
Martez Andrews, II

JOHN LEWIS

May 16, 2016

Mr. Martez Andrews

Dear Mr. Andrews:

It is with great pleasure that I congratulate you on being chosen to represent the State of Georgia as a Delegate at the Congress of Future Science and Technology Leaders.

As a young man, I would hear Dr. Martin Luther King, Jr. speak. I was so inspired to get involved in the Civil Rights Movement. I felt that he was speaking to me. Like he was saying, "You can do it. You can get involved. You must get involved." Even though I was a very young man, as soon as I got the chance, I got involved.

I am proud that you too are getting involved. In addition to the significant work you'll do with the program as a Delegate, I hope you take this opportunity to make your thoughts and opinions known while staying true to your dreams. I believe so deeply in what young people can accomplish because I was personally a part of a group of young people who came together and changed the country.

It is always a joy to see emerging leaders in the making. I am pleased to hear of your record of academic excellence, your leadership ability, and your passion for science and technology. I know that you will represent Georgia well. You never gave up, never gave in. I extend my well wishes and admiration as you continue to make such a positive impact on the world.

Sincerely,

John Lewis
Member of Congress

About the Author

Martez Andrews II is simply a young person trying to make a difference in the world. As he is currently a student at Kenesaw State University, working towards a bachelor's degree in computer science, he will continue to give his best.

He has been interviewed by the Washington Post and has come into contact with many great writers in his endeavors.

His nonfiction books prior to this fiction novel include, *"The Obstacles We Make"*, *"How Peace is Maintained"*, and *"A Legacy That's Shaped."* He enjoys writing and has had many experiences producing quality works for fun and during his educational career.

Some of his hobbies also include photography, art, basketball, programming, and traveling.